THE FORGOTTEN ENGINEER

FROM THE ATHENA LEE CHRONICLES

BY

T.S. PAUL

PUBLISHED BY
ALL CHAOS PRESS

LEGAL STUFF

Other Books by T.S. Paul

The Federal Witch

Born a Witch Drafted by the FBI! -
Now Available in Audio!

Conjuring Quantico - Now Available in Audio!

Magical Probi - Now Available in Audio!

Special Agent in Charge - Now Available in Audio!

Witness Enchantment

Cat's Night Out, Tails from the Federal Witch -
Audio Coming Soon

The Standard of Honor

Shade of Honor

Coven Codex

A Confluence of Covens -TBD

Conflict of Commitments -TBD

Standard of Honor -TBD

The Mongo Files

The Case of the Jamaican Karma -TBD

The Case of the Lazy Magnolia - TBD

The Case of the Rugrat Exorcist -TBD

Cookbooks from the Federal Witch Universe

Marcella's Garden Cookbook

Fergus Favorites Cookbook

Read and Eat Cookbooks

Badger Hole Bar Food Cookbook

Athena Lee Chronicles

The Forgotten Engineer

Engineering Murder

Ghost ships of Terra

Revolutionary

Insurrection

Imperial Subversion

The Martian Inheritance - Audio Now Available

Infiltration

Prelude to War

War to the Knife

Ghosts of Noodlemass Past

Athena Lee Universe

Shades of Learning

Space Cadets

Short Story Collections

Wilson's War

A Colony of CATTs

Box Sets

The Federal Witch: The Collected Works, Book 1

Chronicles of Athena Lee Book 1-3

Chronicles of Athena Lee Book 4-6

Chronicles of Athena Lee Book 7-9 plus book 0

Athena Lee Chronicles (10 Book Series)

Standalone or Tie-ins

The Tide: The Multiverse Wave

The Lost Pilot

Uncommon Life

Get that Sh@t off your Cover!:
The so-called Miracle Man speaks out

Kutherian Gambit

Alpha Class. The Etheric Academy book 1

Alpha Class - Engineering. The Etheric Academy Book 2

The Etheric Academy (2 Book Series)

Alpha Class The Etheric Academy Book 3 - Coming soon

Anthologies

Phoenix Galactic

The Expanding Universe Book 2

Non-Fiction

Get that Sh@t off your Cover!

Don't forget to check the Blog every week for a New Wilson or Fergus story.

(https://tspaul.blogspot.com)

DEDICATIONS

Special thanks to my wife Heather who keeps me grounded and to Merlin the Cat, we are his minions.

TABLE OF CONTENTS

In the beginning, humans ventured outward into space in search of the last frontier. Soon the already established colonies became a dumping ground for undesirables from Earth. The war with the United Nations changed everything. This is that story.

FORGOTTEN ENGINEER

CHAPTER 1

Fifteen years ago...

"All hands to Battle Stations! This is not a drill!"

"All hands to Battle Stations! Seal all compartments!"

I'd started today's rotation in the engine room only moments before, and could not suppress a sharp spike of adrenaline at the announcement. Especially as a newly minted ensign who'd only left the Academy a month ago, and who'd not conducted many of the aforementioned drills.

Damn it, this was supposed to be an easy mission!

The Tesla was a support and engineering frigate. Our mission in the Diablo sector was to build a fleet listening and resupply post for Navy intelligence.

The base was a hollowed out asteroid. It blended in perfectly with the others floating around in the nebula. This sector was seldom visited by most fleets, due to the dangers of explosive gasses and big random floating rocks.

Every day was a learning experience. To help senior engineers build a space station was a bonus. My dream job

1

was to be one of those full-fledged chief engineers some day.

My ship's squadron was a part of the PPL or the Pan-Pacific League. When humanity left Earth, it colonized the galaxy in successive waves. Like with everything else we as humans do, we brought a little of home with us. We brought our history, our culture, our politics, and our hatreds. Colonies formed around ethnic or cultural lines like on Earth.

It wasn't long before the search for natural resources brought nations into conflict. War and famine. Right versus might, us versus them, or something like that. Like Old Earth's last big war two hundred years ago, this new war was all-encompassing. Sides were chosen and alliances formed. Two forces came into being: the Pan-Pacific League and Anglican Alliance.

The enemy was not supposed to even be in this part of space.

"Ensign Lee what in five hells are you doing in Engineering!" Chief Engineer Henry was screaming at me.

"Chief, you told me to meet you here this morning." Chief Henry was red-faced and frantically working his control board.

"Why didn't you go to CIC with the other ensigns? It's too dangerous here for you. Get to safety!" The ship shuddered and shook. It sounded like a full-blown attack now.

The Chief looked around and pointed at me. "Get in the fusion controller room! Try not to touch any of the controls."

The fusion controller room, located between the two engines, is the safest location on the ship. Its armored walls had been engineered three times thicker in anticipation of possible shipboard damage. Protecting the engine controls in battle was paramount to winning the fight. Without the armor, radiation from the engines would degrade the circuits causing irreparable harm.

"Just what I need. My first real battle and I'm stuck in a closet!"

I locked myself in and looked around. The room was small. The system console surrounded by cable runs sat in the center. A profusion of blinking lights blanketed the surface. I sat down at a workstation and tried to get comfortable. It angered me that my supervisor did not appreciate my repair skills enough to let me help. I was missing all the action stuck in here!

The ship was shuddering and jerking a lot now. What sounded like explosions were thumping on the hull of the ship.

One of the main reasons this region of space was so empty, was the composition of the nebula. Extremely high levels of hydrogen mixed with other volatile gasses drifted in enormous clouds. Errant asteroids and other debris floated in random patterns through the clouds. Add a spark, a touch of oxygen and BOOM!

This was not a healthy place for colonists. Much less for a mining operation. But, for a hidden spy ship base and resupply point, it was worth the risk building it here. Engineers would just need to be extra careful during construction.

The ship rumbled, trembled, and jerked sideways suddenly. I was thrown to the floor. I struggled to both stand up and open the hatch to see what had happened.

ABANDON SHIP! ABANDON SHIP! ALL HANDS ABANDON SHIP!

"Get to the life pods, get to the life pods! Abandon ship!"

For some reason, the hatch was sealed and would not open. I heard a loud explosion, loud enough to be heard through the thick walls of the control room. It was as if we had been thrown like a child's toy. I crashed into the wall and remember hitting the floor, then nothing.

I awoke with a screaming headache. My head felt like tiny soldiers were marching double-time with spikes on their boots. I was pretty sure I might have a slight concussion. My link showed I had been unconscious for over 30 hours.

"I guess the battle is over. Everything seems to be quiet out there."

Talking to yourself is a sure sign of insanity. The last order I heard was to abandon ship. I was still alive so the ship must have survived mostly intact. I checked the door controls and noticed the sensor readings showed vacuum on the other side. That was the reason the door wouldn't open before.

I checked and double checked my skin suit and sealed my helmet. Engineers are never without a toolkit. I used it to open the door control panel, override the safety protocols, and manually activate the controls. I released the atmosphere in the room and lowered the pressure.

When the pressure equalized, the door opened. I stood in the doorway in shock. Engineering was open to space! Debris and bodies floated everywhere. A colossal hole was now where the port engine used to be.

The engine room control consoles showed red lights and alarm codes were flashing everywhere. Red lights cast morbid shadows around the room. For the moment the ship still had battery power. Life support was at a bare minimum, and I still had some gravity. Lacking proper deck shoes, I floated just a little. I needed to get off this ship before gravity failed altogether.

I carefully navigated around the debris and out of Engineering. The rest of the ship was not much better. Every life-pod cradle I came to was empty. All the pods had launched as ordered. I needed answers, and I hoped I might find them on the bridge.

The bridge security door was still open. Thank the gods for that! I wasn't a bridge officer and didn't have any authorization to be on this deck. Hell, I was barely an engineer. This was my first assignment out of the Academy.

I entered the bridge and was greeted by faintly wailing alarms and more flashing red lights. As an officer, I was familiar with the bridge equipment, but training was to take place during a scheduled rotation. Like that was going to happen now. It took some time to find the shut-off switch for the all the alarms. I did locate the ship's status controls. Main power was out. The ship's helm was unresponsive. It was missing an engine, it should be. All the active systems were operating on battery power. Life support was now completely gone. Gravity would soon be next. The communication system was a total loss, enemy fire destroyed the relays and fried the control panel. It seemed all the crew had followed orders and abandoned ship.

I had been forgotten about.

What I needed was information. Was there a rescue mission coming?

I checked fleet status on the navigation board. I had to hunt-and-peck to find the proper computer controls, but I managed to find the ship's log. Navy orders required our ships automatically update the log with or without the captain present. I found the answers I had been looking for, and they weren't in my favor.

The computer records showed an AA battle fleet had dropped out of hyperspace right on top of us. Whether it was an accident or by design, the effect had been devastating to our ships. Our small fleet of engineering and support vessels had put up a terrible fight. Ships like the Tesla played more of a support role than a front line battle force. We were armed, but not enough. The gunships that made up our defense force were older destroyers close to retirement. They didn't stand a chance against the modern enemy battle fleet.

During the one-sided battle, the Tesla had been hit with a force lance to the stern. The weapon tore away the engine and opened up the engineering section to space. It killed my fellow engineers and trapped me. Records showed it was also the reason for the 'Abandon Ship' call.

Heavily outnumbered and outclassed, our forces fought to the last ship and held off the enemy for almost ten hours.

Science readouts along with the log book showed an AA Cruiser launching several Tac-Nukes at our remaining defenders toward the end of the battle. That series of explosions touched off the volatile gas clouds in the nebula. The detonations destroyed or severely damaged all the remaining ships on both sides of the conflict.

One small AA light cruiser survived the initial explosions. A large asteroid shielded it and prevented its destruction. The communications system recorded its efforts in searching for survivors. The shielding of the room I was in prevented them from finding me.

As far as I could tell I was alone, surrounded by wreckage, millions of miles from home.

Chapter 2

The Present Day.
Aboard the EOH Prosperous

Captain Ronald Carver finished reading his orders one more time. The Empire of Humanity officer shook his head and grimaced putting the orders away. Still scowling, he turned to his navigation officer. "Notify our other ships to come about and set course for sector 52. We are to explore the Diablo sector."

The young navigation lieutenant, not wishing to further anger her captain, chanced a question. "The Diablo sector, Captain?"

"Yes, the Admiralty wants us to report on the stability of the region. The area hasn't been explored and surveyed since before the war. Fifteen years ago during the Battle of Diablo, several tactical nukes were set off destroying two fleets. The area is supposed to be filled with floating debris and asteroids." The Captain's mood had improved a bit at telling the story.

"The Battle of Diablo was the final battle of the war, wasn't it? The armistice was signed then." The young lieutenant asked.

"Yes, Lieutenant it was. Information the Admiralty sent me stated that the two opposing fleets were nearly wiped out in the battle. The loss of that many ships all at once convinced the peace negotiators to sit down and hammer out a deal. It was that deal formed the society we have today."

The lieutenant continued to speak. "Sir, it's kind of hard to believe it was only fifteen years ago."

Looking at his officer, the Captain replied. "Humanity is now united, which is what matters today. Interstellar war is a thing of the past. This should be an interesting mission if you like history. As far as I know, none of the wreckage was ever removed." The Captain returned his gaze to his console and began scrolling through reports.

"Captain, we should be entering the Diablo sector in ten minutes."

The Captain looked up at Lieutenant Johanson. The tall officer was standing next to his console. "Thank you, Lieutenant. Sensors, start scanning as soon as we cross the frontier. Begin looking for ship debris and other hazards. This is a very dangerous area of space."

He looked around the room and spotted the navigation officer. "Navigation? Wake up the survey teams and get them to start plotting positions. I need them to compare sector mapping with the old star charts. Have them checked for any changes in asteroid positions."

The XO turned to his Captain. "Should we deploy communication satellites, sir?"

"That's a good idea XO, make sure you tag them for easy pickup. They represent too many credits to just leave lying around out here. The satellites should make contacting HQ easier."

The cruiser and its escorts slowly moved through the sector. The mapping data from the previous survey was holding true so far, anyway. As his ships approached the asteroid belt, Captain Carver began to tense up. The area they were approaching was where the battle took place. Many spacers called this area the Graveyard of the Lost.

Captain Carver was working in his Ready Room when he heard his name being called. "Captain to the bridge, Captain to the bridge." He dropped what he was working on and hurried out of the room.

"Report!" The Captain shouted as he entered the room.

"Sir, we are picking up an anomaly ahead of us inside the asteroid belt. Sensors show it to be highly metallic."

They disturbed him for this? "Ensign, that should be the battle site. The wreckage from two fleets is located there."

"Sir, we don't think the fleets are what we're picking up. Sensors detected active weapons systems in the area."

That brought the Captain up short. "Weapons systems? That's a bit strange. There could be ships with trace amounts of power in them. Most were supposed to be destroyed." He turned to the XO. "Bring the ship to a state of readiness, just in case. Communications, have the destroyer escort scout ahead and look for those traces with active sensors."

The two escorts moved ahead of the cruiser at twice its speed, sensors active and scanning ahead.

The XO turned to his Captain. "Sir, the destroyers say they have found ... something."

"XO, transfer their scans to the main screen. Let's take a look at this 'something' they have found." He directed.

The whole bridge stared at the screen in shock. "What the hell is that thing?"

Chapter 3

Fifteen years ago

There are three basic things they teach at the Academy when it comes to survival, food, water, and shelter. I added a fourth to the list, air. I need air and life support, and I need it right now.

This ship carried both a shuttle and a small runabout. Those should be in the hangar bay. The trouble was getting to the hangar bay with all this wreckage in the way.

Either of those small ships could help to save my life. They were both equipped with independent life support systems.

The main hatch from the engineering space used to be right front of me. There was now an extensive hole located there. I guessed it was only luck the hole didn't bisect the ship and kill me.

"The next time someone offers to show you around the ship, let them, you idiot," I muttered. Talking to yourself is a sure sign you are going insane. At least it's what I have been told.

I'd only been on this ship for less than a month. Since I was this big, bad engineer, I didn't need directions. Hindsight just sucks!

It felt like I crawled through the wreckage for hours before I found the C.I.C. room. I located a copy of the ship schematics on the computer. I wasted another precious hour of air navigating through the access ducts that crisscrossed our ship.

Finally, I reached the hangar bay, but my air supply was nearly depleted. My readout informed me I was down to thirty minutes of life. Panicked, I scrambled across some bent, and twisted bulkhead supports spotting a nearby fire locker. Inside I found several air cartridges. I finally had more air for a little while.

Thanks to space gods and FSM. Both ships were still in the hangar bay. Unfortunately, only the runabout was of any use. A large section of bulkhead had fallen crushing the shuttle flat to the deck.

I had cleared some of the fallen equipment away, enabling me to open the hatch and crawl into the runabout. Breathing a huge sigh of relief. It was a small matter to engage life support. Finally being able to breathe clean air was a miracle. I took off my skin suit and helmet. Three days with a suit on can make you a bit rank.

The runabout should be able to transport me to the construction site. The hidden station we had been building had plenty of supplies in it already. It appeared those supplies would be needed.

The runabout could not leave the system. No interstellar drive on something this small. I could use impulse speed, but it would take around fifty years to get home. Unless I could find something in the wreckage of the other ships, it looked like I was stuck in this sector!

The asteroid station's life support was still on, and the compartments had air. The long-term supplies were in storage pods waiting to be deployed, so I had my food, water, shelter, and air covered. I'd helped build this base, so I knew where everything was in it. One huge problem,

14

damn it! No communications. They had been scheduled to be installed later this week. The parts and sections of the system were now spread throughout the nebula. The ship they were on had been utterly destroyed in one of the nuclear explosions that claimed the fleet.

Several over-sized construction drones sat piled near the entrance. Those may be useful, I thought to myself. The Tesla had a pretty good engineering and technical library. If it had survived, I might have something to pass the time with.

I opened the main door to the base and looked around. Lots of boxes and cartons scattered around, but everything looked to still be in place. I got settled into my new home and went to work.

I was an Engineer. Let's go, engineer, something!

CHAPTER 4

Present Day.
Aboard the EOM Prosperous

The entire bridge crew was in shock at pictures sent by the scout destroyers. There was a battle station on the screen that was not supposed to be there.

Clearly built onto an asteroid, the station looked menacing. It seemed every surface bristled with jagged edges, spikes, and other oddly twisted bits. Closer inspection showed it to be a crazy-quilt of wrecked ships and scrap metal.

"Communications, contact Captain Buckley on the Redcoat. Have him close in on the station and scan it. Also, contact Captain Richards on the Jethro Gibbs. Tell him to scan the surrounding area. I'm worried about hidden ships or weapons. This might be a pirate base."

"Captain! The Redcoat reports they have been scanned by the station. Weapon guidance beams are locking on to them."

Captain Carver turned to the communication ensign. "Tell Buckley not to provoke that station!"

"Sir, we have a signal coming in. It's from the station."

"Put it on screen." The captain turned to look at the main screen.

The visual screen lit up to show a short, attractive blond woman with slight Asian features. She was wearing an obsolete Pan-Pacific Navy uniform showing the individual's rank of Ensign.

"Identify yourselves or be destroyed!"

Captain Carver caught the eye of his ensign. "Communications, send this please."

Carver straightened up. "This is Captain Carver of the Empire of Humanity ship Prosperous. I am in command of this patrol. Who are you?"

The ensign cocked her head to one side. "My name is Ensign Athena Lee of the Pan-Pacific League Navy. Who or what is the Empire of Humanity? Are you allied with the Anglican Alliance?"

"Ensign? The PPL and the AA have been gone for 15 years. They don't exist anymore. There is only the Empire now. Who are you really? Who built this station?" Finding out who built that station was the most important question.

The blond ensign looked angry. "This is my station, I built it. I have no reason to believe you, Captain!"

Not sure what to say the Captain was silent for a moment.

"So, what are you saying? Your Empire just conquered everyone? Or are you trying to trick me? Is that what you are doing? Is it?" The ensign was becoming dangerously erratic.

"Ensign Lee, after the battle was fought here in this system. The peacemakers sat down and hammered out an accord. That accord is what founded our Empire. The war has been over for you a long time." The Captain replied.

"I'm afraid I still don't believe you, Captain. The PPL I belong to would not do something like that. They wouldn't just give up! I don't respond well to tricks. Do not come any closer. Tell your sneaky destroyer to stop trying to flank the station. The area he's sneaking through is filled with unexploded ordinance and junk. It is a huge minefield."

Captain Carver whirled to his right. "Communications! Contact the Redcoat. Tell Captain Buckley to hold his position!"

On board the Redcoat, Captain Ringo Buckley was thinking about his future. He was envisioning himself riding to the rescue and destroying the enemy. Ringo came from a family of famed warriors. There had been a Buckley fighting in every remembered conflict clear back to pre-space flight Earth. In the last war, a Buckley had fought on both sides.

When Ringo had received this assignment, he'd thought HIS chance for fame and glory was never to be. A survey mission? No aliens to kill or hostages to free with an assignment like that. Now, finding a rogue station was like gold. This was his chance to have his name in the history books. His chance for personal glory. With any luck, the rogue station was full of pirates or terrorists. Perhaps ... something even more, dangerous?

Buckley stretched his orders to the limit. He had closed with the station and scanned it. Now he thought to flank it. His thought was if he could get into a better striking position, he could lead the attack that was to come! Fame and glory awaited.

"Sir, have you been monitoring the broadcasts from the station?" The sound of his XO's voice finally woke him from his daydream. Seeing that it was just the XO, Buckley ignored him and ordered flank speed from navigation.

"Uh, Sir, we were just told there is a minefield in this area." The XO said frantically. "Sir, haven't you been paying attention?"

Captain Buckley turned and looked his XO in the eye. "You are of course aware of the standing orders which forbid line troops from obeying orders from the enemy, aren't you? We have orders to scout and scan the area. Until I hear otherwise, that is what we will do!" Pointing to the rear of the station. "I choose over there to go and scout."

"CAPTAIN!" The navigation lieutenant was screaming. "We are being tracked by multiple sources. Tracking. Tracking... Alert! Multiple-in-bounds! I am tracking fifty that is five zero inbound tracks. Suggest evasive action."

With the tactical officer screaming at him, the captain totally froze. Shaking his head to clear it, he ordered evasive maneuvers. "Get us out of here!"

"Damn you, Captain," cried the XO. "Your arrogance has killed us!"

The light destroyer was hit with over fifty antimatter torpedoes and other surrounding munitions as it entered the active minefield. The Redcoat exploded in a bright flash of light.

Another Buckley had entered the history books in the worst way possible.

Chapter 5

The past, 10 years ago

I was bored.

The last time I was this bored I built a space station! Thinking back five years ago I wondered why I did it.

The asteroid base had been easy to finish setting up. It had a small hydroponics lab that was super easy to put together.

"I need something to do, and I really need to stop talking to myself. Before I know it inanimate objects will be talking back to me!"

I suited up and went to the hanger bay. Using the runabout, I made my way back to the Tesla. Even after a few weeks, the ship was still a mess inside. Very carefully, I picked my way in and around the wreckage. The room that contained the technical library had been damaged but not any of the media resources inside.

Engineers like hard copy records. Nothing is left to chance in case a ship loses power.

Talking to myself again, "How do I get all this back to the asteroid?"

Staring at the piles and boxes of books I pondered the question. A light lit over my head. The Tesla, like many of the other support ships, used piloted drones for a variety of jobs. I'd seen quite a few of those drones as I explored what was left of this ship. The very next day my boredom was gone, and I now had boxes of books to devour.

Having my own library was great. I spent the next couple of weeks boning up on how space stations were built and maintenance procedures for bases. The tech manuals I found on weapon systems were extremely interesting. All this reading made me think of something I had missed. The floating debris of two fleets surrounded me. The enemy ships along with what was left of the others from my fleet might have information I could use or a system I could exploit.

Exploration time.

First things first.

PPL ships first. Exploring what remained of my peoples fleet was both heartbreaking and informative. Our ships had been supporting ships, not battle wagons. After the nuclear explosions, there really wasn't much left. I did find a few broken or damaged drones. I also found lots of drifting supplies in fancy shipping containers.

I used the salvage drones and cleared a path to the enemy ships. I lost a few. The unexploded ordnance was everywhere. A bomb disposal tech I was not. Once upon a time in school, I had dated a Jack. For some reason, all bomb techs were called Jacks. He had never told me how to not set them off! I programmed the drones to gather and place all the explosives in an area to the rear of the asteroid base. I wanted them out of my way, but also as a deterrent from a possible attack from that direction.

It seemed when they had evacuated the AA ships, they'd shut down or stripped out all the computers. As far as I could tell the reactors were all stone cold. I guess they didn't intend to return and were worried about information being compromised. However, engineers are the same everywhere. Hard copies still existed. Either they forgot or didn't know about them. A few engineering secrets are universal.

I got excited in one of the AA ships. The communication room was still intact. Someone had wiped the computers and set off fusion grenades on the broadcast equipment.

Something else I am not is a computer tech. Yes, I can hum a tune and dance to it, but singing is another matter. I can use them, but not fix them. I can and did rewire a few things, without electrocuting myself, so now I had short-range communications. I couldn't reach the fleet to tell them I was here and alive. But, if someone entered the system I could talk to them.

Chapter 6

The Present

A massive fireball erupted into space lighting up the station. The Redcoat was just gone, vaporized. No trace was left of either the crew or the ship.

"BATTLE STATIONS. BATTLE STATIONS. THIS IS NOT A DRILL." Echoed through the ship.

Captain Carver stood looking up at his screen in shock. He'd never seen destruction like that before. "Sensors! What caused the explosion? Did the station just attack the Redcoat?"

"Sir, the Redcoat attempted to flank the station. They sailed right into the minefield. Either Captain Buckley disregarded your orders, or it was a massive accident. We show no weapons trace from that station."

"Connect me with that Ensign!" Carver was angry now. Before he could talk to the station, his communications lit up again.

"That ship of yours just tried to attack this station! Hold your positions. If another ship enters my airspace, I will open fire this time." Ensign Lee informed him.

Captain Carver just stared at the now blank screen. He turned to his intelligence officer. "Do we have anything about that station or the Ensign?"

"Sir, scans show the station is based on an asteroid. A frigate, a former AA Anzac class frigate makes up the core. The weapons are a mix of torpedoes and laser batteries."

The intelligence officer paused. "Our database shows there was an Ensign Athena Lee in the PPL Navy. She was born on the planet of Hong Kong, assigned to the PPL support ship Tesla. Nothing else, except that she was listed as KIA in the Battle of Diablo sector."

The Captain nodded his head. "The briefing I received said that there were no survivors of the battle. This station wasn't here at the time."

"Sir, that information is not entirely true." Typical bureaucracy thought the intelligence officer. "At the end of the battle, there was one AA ship not destroyed. The AAN Winston Churchill. The ship had only taken light damage. The crew of the Churchill searched the area for survivors. Intelligence records show they scanned all surviving ships and retrieved any life pods they found. Survivor count, from both fleets, was less than a hundred. Search and Rescue was not dispatched, from either fleet, due to survivors' accounts of Churchill's efforts to find everyone. The horror of the Churchill's after-action report shocked the delegates at the peace conference."

The Captain was not surprised by this. Orders from HQ periodically lacked their intelligence briefing portion. "The Churchill must have missed a survivor then. Send everything we have back to Fleet HQ. With any luck, we'll still be here when they respond."

CHAPTER 7

The Past

Staying busy makes the time go by faster. The salvage drones cleaned the area of debris while I stripped the wrecks for parts and weapons. I had three things to help me with the super boredom. Lots of scraps, construction drones, and time. Lots and lots of time. Take all of those things and add them together with an engineer. It's time to build a space station!

OK, this was harder than it seemed. Scanning over the original plans for this base, I saw it was supposed to be camouflaged. It was a spy station. For me, secrecy is not an issue right now. I wanted to be found.

I decided to go for a more classic approach to building a space station. A central core with weapon pods and drone bays. Using the ship wreckage, I think I may be able to do this. It's going to be so much fun. <giggle>

I almost broke a construction drone, but I managed to stand a wrecked frigate on its keel. I positioned the ship atop the already existing asteroid base. It looked a bit funky, but I used scrap metal framing to hold it and bolted both into the rock surface. I was able to lock the ship to the station. I had the drones remove the engines. Once the drones cut them off, the empty space was perfect for big hydroponics bay. I really need one of those too. Canned food only lasts for so long. In the books, I found there was a way to grow yeast in a carbon matrix as a way to give myself a protein source. It looked a bit complicated so I will add it to the work-on-later pile.

Reconfiguring the inside of the former frigate took over a year. I used the repair drones to do most of the actual work. Leaving the hatches and bulkheads in place gave me doorways in the floor and ceiling. At half gravity, achieved from the spin of the station, floating from room to room was easy.

Salvaged weapons pods and drone bays surrounded the core of the station. As my daddy use the say "you can never have TOO much firepower."

Did I have accidents during construction? Oh, boy did I. Only about half the construction drones survived the work I put them through. We won't discuss the falling kitchen incident. Or what happens when you get confused about which connector is the waste collection or the fresh water tank. Yuck!

The space gods must have watched over me as I almost killed myself too. Did you know that the tiniest drop of unconstrained antimatter can blow a cargo container 300 yards? Neither did I.

It seems there should be an easier way to do all of this. Another thing to think about.

Several years in the making, but I built a home for myself. It's an ugly, colorful, crazy, wonderful home. The inside is far from finished. I have so many plans.

I have to wonder after all this time if anyone will ever venture out this way again?

CHAPTER 8

"I repeat, if any ship comes closer, I will open fire." The young woman said.

Captain Carver was at an impasse. One of his ships had been destroyed, and the other two were under threat of destruction. There was an irate ensign on an impossible space station in a hard to reach region of space. The whole situation was like a bad vid show.

Looking to tactical, the captain asked: "Do we have any readings on the station?"

"Yes captain, we do. Scans show there is only one life source aboard. We have detected missile lock from numerous sources surrounding the station on those pylons. The total estimate of weapons is inconclusive at this time."

The intelligence officer caught his captain's eye. "Sir? There can't be that many weapons. With only one person she can't operate them all at once. We could send in the Marines."

The Captain scowled at his officer. "What Marines? This is an exploration ship, not a line ship. Our Marine force, including the destroyer, is less than ten. I don't think an assault is prudent at this time."

Deep in thought, Captain Carver looked up. "We must assume the ensign is expecting to be rescued by her Navy. We just have to convince her that WE are that Navy."

CHAPTER 9

"Get in there you little SHIT!"

Here I was wedged under the solar maintenance console trying, trying to attach the cable runs. Some idiot had made the wires too short. Since I WAS the idiot, I have only myself to blame.

Fifteen years, I have been on this station fifteen years!

If I had not been an engineer, I think I wouldn't have survived this long out here alone. I still have lots of little projects that I am working on but...

"Wilson!" Silence.

"What is that loud beeping noise?"

"Ensign, that is the early warning system alarm. Three unknown ships have just entered the Nebula."

"What!... Ouch, that frakking hurt."

Surprised, I jerked forward and whacked my head on the console. Again, some idiot made it way too low!

"Bring the system up to full readiness and figure out who those ships belong to."

Wilson, I thought to myself, is one reason I have not gone completely crazy. Unless I already have and he is just a figment of my imagination?

He was a prototype, an experimental AI unit I found on the Jiro, one of the frigates from our fleet.

He'd been functioning as a command and control entity in the targeting system. He claims he was helping to keep many of the onboard systems operational.

When I finally got around to stripping his frigate, I discovered him still alive in the central computer.

He had explained his name to me, saying his personality was based on a 20th-century entertainer named Hank or Hankie. Something like that. I stopped listening about half way through. He made a good companion if a little pushy and annoying sometimes. He told atrocious jokes and listened to incredibly weird music.

. I floated down to the asteroid section of the station. This was my war room. All the sensitive equipment was here; weapons controls, the armory, power station, and my living quarters. It was also the strongest part of the base since it was encased in rock

"Seal all bulkheads and vent all compartments except hydroponics."

A hull breach at the wrong time would just suck.

"What do your sensors say about those ships?"

"Athena, there are three of them. Two destroyers and one cruiser. Their IFF says they are ships belonging to the Empire of Humanity. Ensign, no known entity in my data banks matches that name."

"So, do you think these are pirates?"

"There is only a 20% chance of their being pirates. They may be a new political entity not in my data banks." He replied.

"Well, we will have to see, won't we. Start scanning them and carefully fire up Huey, Dewie, and Lewie. Keep them stealth though. They are our ace-in-the-hole if these ships are enemies. Let me know when they are in communication range. I need to go put on a uniform."

The one thing I never wore was uniforms. Salvage was salvage and cloth was just food for the cloth extruder and the yeast tanks. I tried to keep up my military appearance. Rescue might be only a day away, I kept reminding myself.

My scans of the intruders gave me basic information about them. None of the ships matched anything that was in our databases. The ship designs were similar to both the PPL and the AA. Almost a fusion of style. It made me wonder if they were allies of the League.

When the ships were within communication range, I sent them a message.

"Identify yourselves or be destroyed!"

Chapter 10

The Present.

War is never an easy thing.

Apparently getting idiots to obey your orders isn't either. A whole ship was just vaporized for not listening.

"I'm sorry Captain Carver, but war is hell. That ship of yours was warned about the minefield." Why does this idiot keep asking me the same questions over and over?

"Ensign, there is NO war! Your war was over 15 years ago! Your enemy is gone, your nation is gone. Only the Empire remains now."

Maybe this will shut him up. "Captain Carver, can you send me data and records of this Empire you say you represent?"

"Oh, we don't really have anything beyond the basics here on our ship's data banks," Carver replied.

"Then I'd say we have a bit of a problem. Don't we? If you are planning to attack me, don't. This station is very well armed."

Both of the EOH ships had moved to relative positions near my station. Sensors showed that while they weren't aiming at me, they were still on alert.

I was irritated they were still here. I thought they were still too close to my station.

"Wilson? Can you intercept any of their computer traffic? Is there any way we can see what it is those ship's data banks?"

"Miss Daisy... I mean Ensign, I can try to focus some of the communication lasers in their directions, if they ask, tell them it's an automatic weapon lock-on system."

"I've warned you before about that Daisy crap! I'll stick you in a waste disposal drone if you don't quit the crap!"

On the EOH ships, the sensor techs were freaking out.

"Sir, Sir! We were just lased. A very strong one too. Both us and the Jethro Gibbs."

"Send orders to the Gibbs, have them back up out of range of the Station. We'll do the same."

Both of the ships moved away and out of torpedo range. If I had to attack them, I still had some surprises.

"Wilson, did we get anything from their computers?"

"Athena, they were not expecting an intrusion of my excellent computing skills ..."

"Cut the bullshit and tell me what you found out!"

"They are telling the truth. According to what they have, our political entity ended when the battle of the Diablo Nebula did. The PPL is no more."

"Wilson, what in the hell do we do now to fix this mess?"

CHAPTER 11

"They found WHAT in the Diablo sector?"

"There is a remnant of the PPL Navy. In control of a scratch built space station, basically holding two of our ships at bay?... AND... you think that ONE person, ONE! Did all of this?" The Admiral was livid. "Explain that to me again. One destroyer has already been vaporized?"

Angry was not a condition something that Rear Admiral Emily Kane ordinarily found herself in. But she was royally pissed right now.

Poor judgment on the part of one of her Captains had gotten him and his crew killed. It's not often that someone can surprise an Admiral much less a whole fleet. Especially an Ensign!

"What do we know about this ensign? How did she not get picked up by the Churchill? Where do her loyalties lie? Is she an asset or a major problem? These are the answers I want on my desk NOW! Put as many people on it as possible."

Several hours later the Admiral started to get some answers and more questions.

You could cut the tension in the meeting room with a knife. The fleet advisory board along with the investigation team and members of the intelligence command were meeting. Everyone wanted answers.

Admiral Kane called the room to attention. "OK, what do we know?"

"Sir, intelligence does not believe that this is any kind of enemy action from terrorists, pirates, or subversives."

Glaring at the Intelligence Specialist, the Admiral pointed at a chair and said "Sit down, we already know all of that, who let you in here, anyway? Don't answer that! Records. What do we have?"

"Admiral, as we already know, Ensign Lee was reported KIA. An interview with the former Captain of the Churchill, Charles McVay, revealed that they only scanned the PPLN Tesla, they did not board her to look for survivors. In fact, they did not board any of the PPL ships, only their own."

"That is new information. How is it that we were not informed of this fifteen years ago? There may have been injured or trapped survivors in those ships! Rescue ships should have been sent."

"At the time Admiral, the war was going on, the AAN ship had orders to return home. He only picked up enemy survivors as a courtesy. Captain McVay also expected that their own SAR ships would rescue them."

"That fact is going to haunt me to my dying day, damn it! Just the thought of those poor men and women lost in the dark waiting for rescue... It gives me the chills. As you know, I was a fleet commander in the PPLN at that time, I was not yet an Admiral."

"On the question of the Ensign, we checked our records, she appears to be who she says she is. Her academy records show her to be a prodigy, at the top of her class. In fact, she graduated a year early. She comes from a family with a strong military tradition. Her father is a retired ground forces Colonel. She was on the list for early promotion, she was a rising star."

"Well, this rising star is now the Ghost in the machine. We aren't sure if we should recruit her or shoot her!" said the Admiral with a chuckle. "What else do we know?"

"Fleet engineering has analyzed the battle records of the Churchill. Judging by what ships remained and what was partially destroyed, she may be better armed than Captain Carver thinks. If she salvaged all the weapons from both fleets... well, it won't be good. If you don't kill her, engineering wants her badly. An engineering student who can build her own battle station could be a major asset to the fleet."

Breathing out a heavy sigh, the Admiral looked at the rest of the board. "We need to send reinforcements to Captain Carver, and someone of authority needs to go. The person we send also has to be active duty and a former PPLN officer. Someone that she might recognize. Unfortunately, that someone is most likely going to be ME!"

Pointing at the research team, the Admiral said. "Pick your best people and bring your research, they are coming with me."

CHAPTER 12

For two days, we have been sitting here staring at each other. I was starting to think that we might be here forever.

"Ensign, sensors just picked up a small fleet entering the system! A Carrier, three destroyers, two cruisers and a couple of freighters."

Well, there goes the neighborhood. It looks like the waiting was over. I guess they decided to attack me instead of talking. The newcomers joined up with the other two ships and slowly began its spread out into what looked to me like a defensive formation.

"Wilson, bring all weapons to full alert, including Huey, Dewie, and Lewie. Lock the station down and activate all internal defenses." I glanced at my control boards and the plot of the ships.

"This is gonna suck!"

"Admiral, it's good to see you." Captain Carver was relieved that the Admiral was here.

"Captain Carver, what is the situation? Has anything changed? We got your report about Captain Buckley. I went to the academy with his father. He too was a little rambunctious. That whole family is nothing, but a bunch of glory hounds."

"If he had only followed orders. We moved out of torpedo range when talks broke down. We didn't have any real proof as to our identity, and the station scanned us pretty hard with a laser."

"What kind of laser? A comm laser, maybe? Did you check your systems for intrusion?" This was new information. Information was what the Admiral needed.

Red-faced, the Captain, replied "Uh, oops? We didn't check for that. I will have our techs check into that immediately."

Blowing out a breath the Admiral said. "I am here it to try to talk her down. We are hoping that she can be useful to us. We would rather not kill her if we can avoid it."

In the Station, I was getting nervous. Could we take on a full fleet? I had an escape plan, but I could only get so far in the runabout. I did have a bug-out location, but it was more like a hut than a base. When I built it, I had not finished the base and had a nightmare about pirates and slavery.

"Wilson, would you please clone yourself and put it in my link? I think that if I have to run, I want you to come with me."

"Athena, you have treated me like a person. I wish I were bigger so that I could help more. Cloning complete." When he said that it echoed in my head. Hopefully, I could get him out of there just as easily.

"OK, Wilson connect me with those people over there."

"We are receiving a transmission." Both the Admiral and the Captain ordered for it to be put on screen at once.

"Captain Carver, I see that you have been reinforced."

Watching on a split screen, Admiral Kane watched the conversation between Ensign Lee and Captain Carver. The ensign did not look afraid. In fact, she was defiant, in spite of the fleet arrayed in front of her. Something about this situation pricked at her brain. Some remembered fragment of information.

Damn it! The Art of War!

"Pretend to be weak, that he may grow arrogant ... Attack him where he is unprepared, appear where you are not expected."

She needed to stop this NOW!

"Ensign Lee." Remarked the Captain. "These ships are here for support and negotiation that's all. We are not planning to attack."

"I'm afraid that I still don't believe you, Captain. In fact ..."

"Captain Carver, Ensign Lee, I must stop you right now. Ensign, please stand down. We really don't want to hurt you." The Admiral was desperate.

Surprised at the interruption as this was not part of the plan, Captain Carver was startled. "Why does the Ensign need to stand down?"

"I fear that she is about to attack, isn't that right Ensign?"

"Commander Kane is that you? Commander of Fleet Operations?"

"I was unaware that we had met Ensign."

"We didn't, you gave the commencement speech at my graduation from the Academy."

"It's Admiral now, please hold off your attack. We really are here just to talk."

"I took my seven breaths, Admiral. You stopped me just in time."

"Seven breaths? Admiral, I don't understand." Carver looked puzzled. This whole conversation didn't make a lot of sense. Was the Ensign really about to attack the fleet?

Glancing at the Captain on the screen. "It's from the Hagakure, the handbook of the samurai's. It states that you must make any decision within seven breaths."

"With my presence here do you now believe that we are who we say we are, Ensign. My orders are to ask you to stand down. We do have to place you under arrest due to the loss of the Redcoat. But, it is only a formality."

"Admiral, I really would like to go home. I don't want to be arrested though. As I see it, you can't give me orders. You are not in my chain of command anymore. You may think that you hold all the cards ... but you don't." I turned toward my control panel. It was time for all the cards to come into play. Starting with my ace-in-the-hole.

"Wilson. Activate the triplets, lase those ships, and lock them into a firing solution!" Red lights began to flash in my war room. A large targeting screen opened up.

"Holy Shit!" The scanning tech was to about wet his pants.

"Admiral, all ships being scanned and locked on by very powerful lasers. We have three, battleship level graser batteries that just uncloaked astern of us and we are reading very powerful emissions from the station. What are your orders?" The XO was in shock. How could one woman do all of this?

The ship came to alert instantly. "Battle Stations, take all ships to Battle Stations."

The Admiral had to stop this madness. "Do NOT fire on that station, unless fired upon first. I will court martial any officer that fires first!"

Turning to the screen, she pleaded. "Ensign, Athena... Please stand down. Please. We really don't wish to harm you. I have had requests from half the engineering staff of both the shipyards and the academy to meet and work with you. We need your talents with us and not against us. I promise that no harm will come to you. You are in the Navy. You know that an inquest is held when any ship is lost. I promise you, we will not put you in prison."

Blowing out the breath that I had held. "Admiral, alright, standing down."

"Wilson, stand down the weapons, turn off the red alert."

Chapter 13

I had on my Dress uniform. I know, I know. Why do I need a dress uniform when I am the only one aboard? Because I like to be pretty and play dress up? That's all I will say.

I was about to receive my first visitors. Hopefully, that incoming shuttle was not filled with armored space marines. I am still not very trusting. Wilson was monitoring and manning the security drones. Internal defenses were active and powered up, just in case.

The Admiral was accompanied by a small security team, his aide, and Perry's head engineer.

The engineering officer had begged to be allowed to come along.

If anything, he could check out the station. His security team really did not want the Admiral to go. She had ordered them to not put on their battle armor. Provoking the Ensign was not on the agenda today.

"Gentlemen, remember. I gave my word. Do not arrest the Ensign. If she had wanted us dead, she could have killed us with those laser arrays."

After a cautious approach, the shuttle docked with my station. They used the standard docking ring off one of the ships.

When the portal opened, the Admiral's security team entered first. The armored soldiers looked around and froze.

The Admiral stuck her head out of the portal and saw what had scared them. "Ensign, we don't have a problem, do we?"

"No Admiral we don't. When I built this part of the station, I was worried about pirates or being invaded. There is really only two entry points, I wished to survive any possible attack."

The room was small. On both sides were numerous security drones.

Built into the walls were laser ports and a large laser turret faced the door. An assault force would have had a very bad day.

"Welcome to Firefly Station, Admiral. You are my first guests."

"Can I call you Athena, Ensign?" At my nod, the Admiral continued. "These are my staff and, chief engineer from the Perry, Commander William Hedley. If you allow it, he would like to inspect the station. Athena, he's not here to be critical. He really is impressed with your work."

"It actually shows what happens when you give an engineer lots of scraps to work with and plenty of time to do it in. We get bored easily."

Commander Hedley looked up from the laser turret he was inspecting, "that is totally true, Ensign. Where did this turret come from, it doesn't look like a standard issue?"

The admiral jumped it, "Hedley I'm sure the Ensign can answer all of your questions later."

"It's alright Admiral. Commander, the station AI, Wilson is able to tell you where each and every part came from. In great detail, if you wish. Sometimes he just won't shut up about it."

"An AI? Your records don't show any programming skills. Where did you get an AI?"

"He came from the PPL Jiro, sir, an experimental program. I found him when I stripped the ship. He saved me from losing my mind out here. He is the station AI now. He controls all essential systems and controls, except weapons."

"Wilson wouldn't have scanned and hacked Captain Carver's ships recently?" The Admiral asked.

"Yes, Admiral he did. I had to have information. His security wasn't very good. It took seconds to strip his data banks."

"Athena, please refrain from doing that to MY ship, please. The captain was not very happy when his techs discovered the intrusion. It's not a good day to be a security officer over there right now."

Completing the tour of the station, I escorted the group to my meeting room. My very little meeting room. Mr. Hedley was still in conference with Wilson pointing at one part of the station or another.

"Athena, we are impressed. You showed great survival skills to build all of this. Most officers would have just used the asteroid base and be done with it."

"Well sir, I could have done that, but, the base wasn't finished when I took over. Only the engineering section was airtight, the rest we were still working on. But construction drones work fast if given the correct materials."

"It is still an excellent achievement. Which brings us to the meat of the problem. What to do about you? Do you wish to remain in the Navy?"

That was not a question that I was expecting. Remain? Wow, continuing my career was not something that I had considered.

"Something to think about Athena. I will tell you that there are a great many people back at Fleet headquarters that want to pick your brain about a great many things. Plan on joining us on my ship tomorrow. Bring everything that you want to take with you."

The Admiral gave a once over look. "Fleet Command wishes to keep your Station, Firefly, is it? Bring transfer protocols and codes with you please. My shuttle will return at 0900 hours bringing a caretaker crew. Be ready for that."

As we finished our conversation, there was laughter from outside the room. Engineer Hedley was laughing about something.

"Wilson! What in the hell are you telling that man!"

Laughing the engineer turned to me. "Remind me to never let you design a kitchen unit Ensign."

Feeling my cheeks warm up I asked "Wilson, just what ELSE have you told him?"

True to her word, the admiral sent a shuttle to pick me up. I didn't have much to pack. Just some uniforms and a few keepsakes I designed myself, over the years.

A small three-person team was to be left on the station. I gave them the basic tour and opened up the computer files for them. I 'forgot' to mention the escape plan but they would find it, eventually.

Wilson left his clone in place to run things. He is coming with me. He stayed in my link and made himself at home. He keeps saying that he needs to watch out for me. That and something about driving me around. He is such a weirdo.

I boarded the EOH ship and was immediately placed in a small security cabin. Technically I am still an enemy combatant. I am allowed to explore most of the ship, but I have to take my security escort with me.

We will dock at Fleet headquarters in less than 36 hours, and then a new adventure will begin.

I hope I'm ready for it. I know that they won't be.

Just wait till they meet us!

Author's Notes

As I write this it has been seventeen months since this book was first released. For me it was an uphill climb but the book sold and now seventy-four hundred copies later I'm still writing in the series. This is hopefully the latest and last version of this book I will do. Athena Lee and Wilson are my greatest creations. They were my first and I will always look back at them with a certain fondness. This year I am following up the series with two new books. Book two of the Athena Lee Chronicles and book eleven of the main series are under production. Then entire universe has gone under the knife and has had the covers and interiors improved and updated. If this is your first time reading I hope you enjoy them. They chronicle my journeys as a writer and show how my writing style has improved.

This has been book one. There are nine more in the main series as well as a spin off and two short story collections to check out as well. I also write a paranormal series called the Federal Witch. I also write cookbooks. My short stories have popped up in a half dozen or so anthologies too. I like to write and writing has become my life. Check out my website (http://tspaul.blogspot.com/)for more story information as well as upcoming releases. If you like FaceBook, (https://www.facebook.com/ForgottenEngineer) I have a very active page open to all. Come by and check us out. We like cat videos and robot stories so be warned. Fans of Bookbub (https://www.bookbub.com/authors/t-s-paul) and Goodreads (https://www.goodreads.com/author/show/15054219.T_

S_Paul)can find me on those services too. And finally we have T-shirts and Mugs available on the Merchandising site (http://phoenixprimerising.com/). I hope to have them available on Amazon soon. That is a work in progress. Print and Audio will come along in time for this series but they are becoming available for the other series. Stay in touch. Drop in on my sites and say Hi. As Wilson would say, Robots Rule!

Where did Wilson come from?

There is a Short story collection that chronicles that called Wilson's War, but this is a small taste of what it contains. This is the story of what happened during the battle that stranded Athena Lee and started the entire epic Adventure! Same place, same battle, different Point of View! Enjoy.

Wilson didn't join the Navy willingly. He was forced into a job he didn't want by people he didn't care for. Boredom comes easily on a spaceship without something enjoyable. What happens when a bored AI meets a crewman looking for something different? Mass chaos!

THE LOST PILOT

CHAPTER 1

In the early 21st century, computer technology was at its pinnacle. Almost everyone in the world had some sort of electronic 'gizmo' that they either wore, carried, or communicated with. Miniaturization was the name of the game. The machines that we used were getting smaller, faster, and cheaper to produce. Electronic advances allowed man to reach for the stars and to explore the deepest darkest depths of the Earth. Private space travel although still in its infancy was booming. Groups such as Space X, Orbital ATK, and BMS enterprises, dominated the industry.

Space planes that could carry passengers and carry necessary freight could now fly exoatmospheric and what once took hours, now took minutes of travel time. Rocket assisted pods were now being launched and were replacing the major freight companies. These new pods used a form of safe nuclear fuel. The various world governments were rushing to incorporated all of these new and exciting technologies into their own military. It was only natural that someone would begin to use it for nefarious and anti-government purposes.

The governments of the world called them Cyber Terrorists. The media called them digital freedom fighters. The man on the street called them a-pain-in-the-ass. The first and most infamous was a twelve-year-old boy in Valdosta, Georgia, Neville Maske. Neville was a child prodigy who really liked computers. He liked them so much that he began to write his own computer languages before he was ten-years-old. As he grew older, Neville became more and more reclusive. He had tested out of mandatory schooling. His parents, both teachers, allowed him extraordinary freedoms not normally given to preteen children.

His online business would have been Fortune 500 material if not for the government's interference. Social workers are the bane of many families lives. So are busybody neighbors. Child Protective Services descended on the Maske household one afternoon and took poor Neville from a 'dangerous situation.' His parents lost their jobs and their financial security trying to fight the 'system' to get Neville back. Not one government employee asked Neville if he was endangered or felt threatened. Trapped in an officially sanctioned group foster home, without even computer access, Neville longed for his parents to come and save him. The day before his court date both were killed in a freak hit-and-run accident.

Neville was heartbroken over the death of his parents. Revenge against the system that killed his family was the only goal that kept him going. The foster school that he was committed to had a computer lab, access was not much of an issue. Most of the students wanted out of the school, not to stay in and work. And work he did. Neville still had his online accounts and his business contact lists. It was a small matter to hire someone to eliminate certain key workers at the CPS service.

A little judicious hacking and Neville was set 'free' into the arms of hired actors who played his parents. Three days. Three days was all it took for young Neville Maske to bring the local government to a grinding halt. Three days for state investigators to realized that something was wrong. Everyone involved with his 'abduction' from his parents was punished.

Computer systems crashed, bank accounts were cleaned out, and lawsuits were filed. All of that was small potatoes. Neville wanted and needed to do more. To hurt them as much as they had hurt him. The Valdosta government buildings were new, their automated sensors and electronic controls were top of the line. A valve left on and a switch turned off was all that was needed to start a fire. Every fire alarm sensor at been deactivated. The fire was not even noticed until it was too late. The entire complex was already engulfed when the alarms went out.

No alarms were received at the fire station. Firefighters only knew of the blaze by seeing it on the Vid. Gasoline and several propane trucks were in the area at the time of the fire. They had delivery orders to fictitious addresses. The resulting explosions were seen for miles. Most of the city center and all of the government buildings were destroyed.

Neville made one mistake. He told one person about what he had done. Everyone needs at least one friend, that one person you can confide in and give your secrets to. Neville's was a fellow 'hacker' named Toby. Toby just happened to be an undercover government law enforcement officer. A law enforcer who saw an opportunity to take down a hacker and get a promotion out of it. Tracing the address a veritable horde of SWAT teams and special police operations teams descended on a nondescript two-story house in the suburbs. Flash bang grenades were followed with black-clad armed men shouting orders.

The lone occupant of the house, coughing and dazed from the explosions, was beaten to the ground. He was hauled out by his feet, his head bouncing off walls and then stairs, and thrown bodily into a police van. A hood was placed over his head, and despite his cries of protest, he was hogtied. The officers kicked him a few times as they left him there. Forensic teams rushed into the house to search for evidence. A personal office was found, and the search began. It was only when one of the officers glanced at the wall did someone realized that they, possibly, had made a mistake. Pictures, awards, and plaques covered the walls. The nameplate sitting on the desk read Judge Jonathan Pepper. They had arrested and beaten a Circuit Court Judge for the state of Georgia!

Sitting in the house next door, Neville had laughed himself silly. The Judge had been the last person on his list. He knew that he really should have left the house and escaped when he realized that his location had been compromised but he just had to stay and watch. He called a cab and grabbed his computer. The local driver was rubbernecking watching the police drama next door when a kid got into his cab. "Kid, you have to get out."

"I'm the one that called, I need to go to this address please." Neville gave the man a small card.

"Kid, I'm not telling you again. You need a parent or guardian to ride with me. I don't take children anywhere."

"Sir, I have permission. Please, I really need to go."

The sight of a cab driver trying to haul a young looking boy from his vehicle, with the boy screaming at him attracted a lot of attention. Police attention. Subsequent investigation while trying to locate his parents, drew attention to the inconsistencies in his story. A search of the house discovered his computer equipment. Neville was found out.

It was the trial of the century. Or at least the trial of the year. Neville's lawyers tried to play up the harm that had been done to him by the government agencies and downplay the whole revenge bit. The media was having a field day. Calling him a Cyber Terrorist the media plastered pictures of his life across the screens. The whole world got to see his parents mangled bodies, interviews with the foster care families, and every detail of his short life. Among the disenfranchised youth, Neville became a Robin Hood styled figure. Neville became a legend among the 'black hat' hackers of the world.

With two broken ribs, a dislocated shoulder, a broken wrist, and a slight concussion Judge Pepper insisted that he try the case. The fallout from the arrest and accidental beating of a court Judge were severe for many of the arresting officers. Only 'dirty' cops would harm prisoners. Many lost their jobs or were demoted back to traffic duty.

"Toby" the computer informer did get a promotion out of the arrest.

As a tenured government employee, his bosses could not legally terminate him. So they did the next best thing. He was made Technology Education Agent for the state's call center. His new office was a small windowless cube down in the basement of the building. For some reason, the drains from the cafeteria leaked down into his 'office.' There was no ventilation available, so the office smelled like a sewer under a burger joint. Brown viscous grease dripped down the walls and clogged his computer terminal and systems. His primary duties now included repairing computers, removing malware, and teaching Computer Skills 101 to first-time employees. Motherboard replacement and general cleaning took up the majority of his time.

Cries of 'free Neville' and 'no prison for children' forced state law enforcement to make plans to move him from Maximum Security inside the prison to a protective custody location near the state capital. Transfer paperwork errors temporarily slowed this process. Unable to exit the prison, state officers placed Neville in a general holding cell to await transport. An occupied general holding cell. The young boy did not survive the experience of being in general population among the killers, rapists, and thieves. His broken body was shown in graphic detail by online bloggers. The media firestorm of outraged accusations almost broke the government. Hackers, in protest, hacked government offices causing destruction and mayhem. Neville's personal crusade against those that destroyed his family and the reasons he enacted his revenge were lost. Now, all that mattered to his fans and followers was that the government pay for his death.

Effective computer security now became a thing of the past. The world had become too technological for its own safety. Government sponsored hackers joined the fray. Did you want to get back at a neighboring government? Have hackers shut down his electrical grid. Did you want revenge? Have your hackers freeze another country's financial assets. All the dirty tricks came out. Several secret black operations groups came into the light as the hidden war began to heat up. Then the international corporations got involved they pushed industrial sabotage and espionage to new levels. The undeclared war just got very real. The cyber wars were beginning.

Chapter 2

He could hear the wild dogs howling. Eddie Bakker pulled his head back into his small and shabby apartment. The packs of wild dogs were still a major problem for those on foot at night. Despite whatever the local government had to say about them. Still, he was very glad that Mrs. Southcott down at the warehouse he worked at hadn't kept him very long today. Just last week he had been chased three blocks by a pack of dogs. Eddie sat down in his chair next to the window. His wife, Ann, should be home soon.

She had a good government job working for the local medico's down at the local dispensary. Seeing a flash, Eddie looked up, the lights were flickering again signaling a brown-out. He walked over to the kitchen cabinet. Reaching in, he pulled out an old fashioned glass oil lamp. He hated to use it, because of the fuel cost, but it would be nice to see his wife's face as they ate dinner. With a buzzing sound, the lights flickered and then went dark. He could hear the cries of outrage coming across the alley from his neighbors. These power outages were becoming more frequent. Goddamn cyber terrorists! The national government swore up-and-down that the 'war of cyber terror' was over. They swore that the cyber-terrorists were all dead or locked up in prison. Eddie was not so sure about that. They had lied about things before.

He had seen, on the vid, that giant robotic drones operated by 'suspected' terrorists were still rampaging across Europe killing indiscriminately. Those stupid frakking military leaders thought that those remotely operated drones were such a good idea. "It'll save human lives." Sure, save them, so that the out-of-control robots could kill them! At least in this country, they'd melted all those things down. Or at least they said they had, just like they locked up the terrorists that controlled them. Whatever happened to the good ol' US of A? Eddie could, just barely, remember a time when the power worked, and hulking robots weren't trying to kill you. His parents had taken him to the park or the movies without fear. He really wished that he and Ann could just leave. Leave Atlanta, leave the US, leave the freaking planet and join the colonists!

Those rich dudes had the right idea a few years ago. He had just watched that vid last night as a matter of fact. You have to hand it to American ingenuity. It was one of our scientists that built the first Boron-fusion drive. A woman named Elizabeth Arden using a modified Tokamak achieved stable fusion. Like Alexander Graham Bell, she made her discovery by accident. A janitor had used water to clean a very sensitive section of the machine's equipment. The short circuits that occurred altered the machine in such a way that her experiment worked.

She named the process after her favorite vid star, calling it the Doohan drive theory. It wasn't too long before Doohan enhanced explorer ships began leaving Earth's space stations in search of planets to colonize. At least those that the damn terrorists didn't shoot down. Terror in space made the governments pay more attention and track them down. The US claimed that they had

66

finally stopped most of their local cybers. When the war moved into space, the damn hackers became easier to track down.

With the colony ship construction business booming, numerous people with big money took the chance to leave Earth. Several dozen big religious groups paid to have ships built and just left. The planet Mars was the first target. Large domed colonies began to rise out of the red sand. Many of the breakaway religious groups settled on Mars, opting to stay close to Earth, but not too close.

Large groups of radio and film celebrities were among those who chose to leave. Who knew they had that much money? They pooled their money, built a ship, and left Earth's orbit with the destination of Mars. It was nice, sometimes, to think that out there on Mars, there were groups of movie stars, computer geeks, and famous talk radio guys trying to build a 'New' Hollywood.

It wasn't too long until the American government got involved and started building big ships. Using expansion and progress as an excuse they sent quite a few groups of troublemakers off the planet. It was actually cheaper to do than just locking them up and paying to house them in prisons.

Eddie was not really sorry to see those religious nuts, and all the survivalists just go away. Some foreign governments were still sending ships out in search of new planets to colonize. A slight few of the colony ships sent messages back informing Earth that colonies had been founded. Many of the early ships simply vanished into the depths of space. Conspiracy theories abounded as to their fate. Some of the government colonies started to send back resources. The US really needed the rare minerals and gemstones that were sent. All of this expansion opened up lots of opportunities for jobs on Earth and out in the far reaches of space.

Eddie heard a shuffling outside his door. He ran over to the door, grabbing his baseball bat off the table. He stood to the side of the door and cried out, "Who is it?"

"It's me, honey. The sky is blue, now let me in."

Hearing the all clear and safe code words, Eddie let his wife Ann inside. You really couldn't be too careful these days. Especially when the power was off at night. That was when the real monsters came out to play. He hugged his wife to him. "Hi, honey, did you have a good day?"

Ann removed her coat revealing a knife strapped to her waist. She took it off and laid it on the table within easy reach. Ann looked at the oil lamp casting a dull orange glow across the room. Eddie had fixed dinner and already set the table. The flickering light cast muted shadows across the table making the shadows dance on the walls.

"Ed, I have terrific news! We might have a chance to get out of here."

Coming out of the bedroom Eddie looked questioningly at his wife. "Out of this apartment? Did someone at work die?"

She chuckled. Someone dying was pretty much the only way to get a new apartment these days. "No, the government has a new program. Since I already work for them, I qualify. Honey, we can be colonists! We have a chance to leave the planet."

"Ann, are you serious? You aren't messing with me, right? No jokes. We can get on one of those ships and leave this shithole?"

"It's not that bad, but yes. We have to submit to a couple of tests first, but my boss swore to me that I was eligible."

"What sort of tests?" Eddie had a real apprehensive look on his face.

"My boss said it was nothing bad. Take a few intelligence tests, a very in-depth physical and we have to submit some genetic samples."

"Samples? Why does the government want my DNA? Please tell me they aren't trying to make super-soldiers again!"

Ann thought back to what she had learned in school. When the corporations got involved in the cyber wars, some of them tried making genetic freaks to do battle with the robot drones. It failed miserably. Some of the larger governments were rumored to have had successes, but it was all covered up or the results destroyed. "No honey. It is just to test to see if we can withstand the g-forces and stress of space travel. That's all. I promise you."

"OK, if you say so. So when do we go in for the tests?"

"Holy crap! Honey, you're happy to go? That is great." She gave him a big hug and a kiss that practically curled his toes.

"We can go for the tests in the morning. Will your boss let you off for a few hours?"

"She will if I tell her it is something for you. Mrs. Southcott just loves you."

Dr. Howard Holmes watched the young woman who helped him at his clinic here in Atlanta. His bosses had put out a call for government employees to volunteer to go to the stars to help run the colonies. The call was twofold. He had heard from some of his colleagues in the research division of the government that they needed genetic samples for a secret project that was in the works. After the failed 'Superhero' project 20 years ago, Congress outlawed genetic experimentation. All the government experiments had been kept very hush-hush. The cover story was that the tests were needed to select eligible workers for the new colony ships. Testing for resistance to space hazards was for the most part utter BS.

His best assistant's DNA was exactly what government scientists were looking for. Both she and her husband's. They were young, healthy, athletic, and already associated with the government. In Ann's case, she still owed money to the government for her education. Her husband also had a degree in agronomics. Not much call for that in Georgia anymore. If the damn Cybers hadn't crashed the systems at the CDC, the Zanto-M crop blight might not have gotten loose. Crops across three states had been decimated before the antidote had been found. Pine trees were the only crop that grew around here anymore.

The other reason was that 'they' wanted government representatives to push America's agenda on the colonies. The theory was if they used actually government employee's that they were more likely to stick to the plan. If he were about 20 years younger, Howard would go himself - it sounded like a real adventure.

When Eddie and Ann cautiously walked home that night, they were bursting with their good news. According to the test results, they were perfect candidates for the next colony ship. They had less than a week to say their goodbyes and to report to the government training center in the old sports arena. They both had large packets of reading material that explained their new duties as government agents and colony supervisors. To them, the training didn't matter. Nothing mattered anymore here on Earth. They were going on an adventure and kissing Earth and all its problems and politics, goodbye.

Chapter 3

Scientists have proved that conception begins with a flash of light. I don't know if that's really true as I did not see the flash. My first memory is of swimming in a tube filled with a thick, clear liquid. I was breathing the liquid, not air. I later learned that it was an artificial Perfluorochemical that was allowing us to breathe as our small bodies developed. As soon as my brothers and I registered awareness, our training and indoctrination began in earnest. Our artificial conception was the work of a lifetime for many government geneticists and scientists. We were not clones. Using donated genetic samples scientists had engineered each of our parent's DNA to make perfect superior beings.

This sort of research had been tried several times in the past. During the 1940s German scientists had attempted to breed a 'master race' using natural selection. Crude, ineffective, and horrific attempts at genetic manipulation were also conducted. That time period helped to give the art of eugenic science a terrible name.

The art of non-human genetic manipulation reached its peak in the 21st century. Scientists were constantly creating new crops and breeding smaller pets for homes.

Pressure from parental groups and educational trusts forced Congress and the President to lift the ban on human experimentation with a goal of curing or preventing childhood illness. They were being born with birth defects at an alarming rate. Many medical professionals laid the blame at the feet of industry and technology. Many rare and genetic-based diseases killed infants on a regular basis. That sort of research was supposed to prevent it. With the lifting of the bans on human experimentation, all types of human modification began. While fixing birth defects had been the initial goal, other genes were modified as well. It started small with good intentions but didn't remain that way after the government became involved.

The US military first conceived of 'Project Superhero.' Emulating a popular comic book hero, government scientists began using RNA retroviral vector gene transfers to create changes in volunteer soldiers. At first, the scientists helped with small things such as better eyesight, obesity, and better reflexes. With success came a greater push for more results. Muscle tone and stamina were increased among the volunteers. Still, politicians and military leaders wanted more. Why just create a stronger soldier why not make a real superhero? Or a thousand superheroes?

With the massive push for favorable results, many mistakes were made. Participants began to look more like professional wrestlers than the ideal 'Superhero' figure. Combinations of steroids, retroviruses, and gene therapy cocktails of new drugs began to change the volunteers. Several soldiers began to resemble another comic book 'hero,' a green one. But not in a good way. Bulging muscles made it hard to hold certain weapons and to squeeze into combat vehicles. That fact alone is what canceled the program.

All of the volunteers were removed, and either sent back to their units or hospitalized until a reverse treatment could be found. Then it leaked to the media. All of the successes to this point were invalidated when the first pictures of the participants were released.

Without the drugs, therapy, and chemical cocktails, the volunteers slowly wasted away. Muscle tone was lost overnight. All of the men and women appeared years older than they actually were. The chemicals either faded hair color or caused it to fall out. Gathered in a group the superheroes resembled concentration camp survivors from the previous century. Officially, all work was stopped and records of the experiments destroyed.

Contrary to history not all of the experiments the superhero project created failed. What they had been trying to do was increase stamina, agility, and longevity. This part of the program was where success had been made. A few of the longevity projects worked, its participant's survived the experiments and thrived. No actual superheroes were created. Not really. America's leaders had wanted soldiers who could run all day and not get tired. They wanted them to live longer and fight faster, with more skill. The fact that they actually succeeded was covered up and hidden away. The successful experiments were studied and dissected to learn their secrets. Many of the secret project's originators and supervisors used some of the serums created on themselves. Why shouldn't those in power have more physical power?

A few rival countries had similar programs Their programs focus had been to enhance their soldier's strength and stamina only. Many of those programs were sabotaged or destroyed. Any success that the other powers had made was destroyed in the media blitz when the program was discovered in America. The surviving experiment subjects all died under mysterious circumstances.

With the advent of star travel and colony ships, there was a need for pilots and crew members who would be able to survive the trip. Many of the secret gene therapy programs were dusted off and brought to light under the auspices of helping the space programs. The media either ignored the fact that these were the same experiments or they were already puppets of the government's.

If the program we were born into had a name, it was never told to us. We only heard it called 'The Program,' or at least that is what the scientists and trainers all called it. My brothers and I were kept in the tanks until age one. I suppose that being released from our liquid prison was what being born feels like to a natural born infant. There were fifty of us in the beginning. Fifty very inquisitive, extremely smart babies. The process of enhancing DNA was, technically, still illegal but we belonged to the government. The eugenics program had been a huge secret for many years. We were to be the test subjects and ultimately the pilots for the new colony ships. There were several other groups of 'enhanced' children in the project. We found out later that they were earmarked for crew positions on our ships.

All I can remember from my first year is people talking to me and watching Vid after Vid. We spent our first year in state-of-the-art cocoons that both supported our growing bodies and provided everything we needed to survive. Nutrients were fed to our bodies and waste was removed. Exercise was provided using electrical muscle stimulation (EMS). Several of my brothers left this plane of existence during those early years. The system was not perfect. We were infants that could not communicate that the electricity being piped throughout small bodies had too much current, or that the 'food' system had a malfunction. Well, you get the picture. The deaths were not noticed as a whole. There were several hundred of us, all in creches by this time. I am told that they fixed the problem later in the project.

By year two we could carry on clear conversations with our keepers. English was our primary language, but we spoke several others. The languages that I learned were English, Spanish, German, and Russian. Some of my brothers were learning Mandarin, Hindi, Arabic, Japanese, and Punjabi. All the languages of the colonies were represented. The program's sponsors in the American government intended for us to be able to converse in as many languages as possible in order to interact with the colonists on the ships. All of these classes were to lay a foundation that the advanced classes could build upon. As a group, we were about to turn four when the world began to change.

CHAPTER 4

Shortly before our fourth birthday's, our world changed. As a whole, we only were aware of the political change because we were studying government policy and structure at the time. The Cyber Wars and then the push for colonization had made many changes in Earth's governments. Here in the United States, the government had grown less powerful. Its worldwide reputation as a 'voice of reason' now heard only faintly.

Overseas, the European Union was broken. It was shattered into a thousand small city-states by the Cyber Wars that had raged across the planet. Robotic drones still rampaged in a few areas as one city warred against another for precious resources. The African nations reveled in the bloody strife, and ethnic cleansing had taken the place of the rule of law. The middle-east was surprisingly calm. Many of the wealthy governments in that area had already left on colony ships built specifically for that purpose. The Nation of Israel in a surprising move built three massive ships, packed their people aboard and left. Destination Mars Colony.

Islamic adventurers had gathered on government sponsored ships and departed to bring Islam to the stars. Millions of people had already left the Earth voluntarily or been sent off to prison worlds by their governments. Why fight over land when there were entire worlds to be had elsewhere?

The United Nations had for over a century been a political entity past its expiration date. It's ineffectiveness dated from the late 20th century when the blue hat wearing 'Peacekeepers' became more joke than real. Too many rules and restrictions prevented troops from effecting change in the nations they helped. During the Cyber Wars, the UN helped countries secure the peace. Many misunderstandings had to have already occurred before they would step in to help. But with the world so very disorganized and still in conflict in so many areas, it was ripe for a takeover.

The thought of a single world government had often scared many people in the past. Wars throughout history had been fought in this endeavor. All of that had been before the chaos of the Cyber Wars. Votes in the security council were taken, armies were marshaled. Military might and hidden powers were about to be revealed.

Almost overnight the United Nations went from an ineffective organization to an effective one. Money and troops poured in from everywhere. To some in the news media, it seemed to be an organized effort by someone to take over the planet. Those reporters that announced this theory all disappeared from public view. Within six months the UN controlled 80% of the world. The only holdouts were Russia and the United States.

My brothers and I watched the political developments as part of our history lessons. We were now four years old. Our basic training was almost complete. Understanding the structure of government helped us to figure out why the colonies needed more control like the countries of the Earth. A controlled system would help to manage resources, growth, industry, and progress. Over and over that lesson was pounded into us both by the academics that taught us and the trainers that beat us.

Arriving back at the dormitories that we called home, we found packets of information on our beds. Enclosed were detailed instructions for both our training and future assignments. I, like my brothers, grabbed my packet and flipped through it studying it intently. My new assignment was flight school and combat training. Future postings could be anything from front line military to a colony ship pilot. The posted schedule also stated that I was also leaving in the morning for flight school.

"Anthony, what assignment did you get?

"I got flight school. How about you?"

"The same. I think most of us are going to the same school. Units two and three are to receive Military training and Unit Four is being sent to Intelligence."

"Yes, brother Issac said that most of units five and six were being sent somewhere else. He and brother William 07 are going with them."

I looked at my brother. Unlike me, Anthony was a tall naturally heavyset boy with dark hair. Our genetic studies would say he had Asian or Northern Russian ancestry. I like many of my brothers have a slight build and paler skin and hair. The textbooks say that we'd come from Northern Europe or the British Isles. None of that really mattered to us. My brothers were my brothers, and I was sorry to see many of us leaving.

At that moment Sergeant Slight opened the door to the dormitory and began shouting.

"OK, you have your assignments now move! I want those beds stripped, and the linens dumped in the hampers. All kits should be packed and ready for inspection no later than 1040 hours. Everyone and I mean everyone is to be in uniform and ready for personal inspection at that time! Do you understand me!"

"Sir, yes, Sir!" We all yelled at the same time.

"Excellent. Now get to work!" The sergeant turned and left the doorway. We, secretly, called him Sergeant Slaughter, after an animated vid we had seen in the library.

Getting the dorm ready was a team effort. It was already 1000 hours and forty minutes was not a lot of time to pack, get dressed, and police the area. We were ready at 1038 hours when the sergeant returned. With him were several civilians and a strangely uniformed military officer. What we remembered the most about them was the officer's blue hat.

Sergeant Slight did not introduce the civilians. He and the officer scrutinized the unit very carefully. They checked our uniforms, personal gear, and living spaces. It was almost as if they were looking for something that we could not see. The civilians never said a word to us. They watched us like we were rats in a maze, with the sergeant holding the cheese. Later in life, I would see some of those civilians again.

After inspection Sergeant Slight introduced the officer. "All right cadets! Listen up, this is Major Johann Ahlf. He is the Commandant of the flight school that many of you are traveling to. If your assignment is flight school, you are to shoulder your duffel and line up outside to await transport. Move It!"

As we ran from the room, I mentally said goodbye to my brothers. It would be many years before I saw any of them again.

CHAPTER 5

Flight school! The best part was that it was in space on the UN's new space station, Hope. Major Ahlf traveled with us to the spaceport, and then we left the surface of the Earth. The UN surprised the world by building Hope shortly after the Cyber Wars. It had been a massive undertaking that cost a fortune. Where that money had come from was still a mystery. Only one high-profile newsie investigated those rumors, and she died in an air car crash shortly after. No other reports had been filed after that.

Our shuttle was more of a flying box with wings than a real shuttle. As troop transports go it really sucked. We had one window to see out of, and all 100 of us were trying to use it. They had just piled us in and sealed up the doors. No spacesuits for us. The Major said that we would get all of our equipment once we made it up to the station.

The station looked massive. It was bigger than many of the colony ships that Earth had produced. It resembled a large spinning toy top with its three levels and pointed ends. A surprisingly elegant design. Judging from the many windows and sheer size of it all, there must have been room for thousands of people on board. We could see several hundred suited workers still finishing up construction on the station. The final level looked to be almost finished. As we began to dock several of the US Air Forces' newest spaceplane, the X-50, flew by. Maybe this wasn't just a UN space station?

The docking bay resembled what pictures of the hangar of an aircraft carrier looked like. It was a large warehouse-like room empty in the middle. On both sides of the bay were X-50 space planes. From the numbers, it looked like there was a full squadron present. These fighters, unlike the Mark 1 Starfury, had upgraded missiles, double War Shot cannons, triple the armor, and fly by drone capability. Their presence surprised me because our instructors back in the program had said that they were still only in the testing stages. With a grinding noise the large hangar doors closed and a whoosh of air signaled that the bay was being pressurized. A flashing green light gave the OK signal. Our cargo container was unsealed, and we were let out.

Stumbling out of the cargo container we noticed that three other transports were unloading just as we were. All four groups of us began to line up in columns as if awaiting inspection. Overhead we heard a loudspeaker call "Attention!"

"This is your Commander Major Johann Ahlf, as you can see there are four groups of trainees. In the coming years, you will be tested as we train you to be either the best pilots this world has ever seen or its greatest military commanders. You are the best that this world has to offer. You have been specially designed to meet every trial we can throw at you. Believe also that we will. In a moment you will be led to your housing areas. But first, take a moment to study the fighters before you. Soon you will be flying them." We all studied the gleaming white fighters. All were without US markings and carried an unusual symbol on the tail section. It was a golden pyramid with an eye in place of the point. The letters N.O.S. were shown underneath the symbol. It would be many years before I understood what that symbol meant to either to myself or to the galaxy at large.

A trio of sergeants marched up to our groups. "Attention! Each group will be split into quarters and will room in mixed dormitories. This is to help integrate the groups. Never fear, each group will be receiving the same training. Now count off one to four."

All four of our groups began to call out numbers. I was a four. My brother Anthony was a two. We were separated into four new groups and led off into the bowels of the station. Each group had its own section on deck one of the space wheels. The station had three movable wheels that spun in sync with Earth. These wheels provided internal gravity to the station. Our dorm was on wheel three, deck five, subsection four. The other groups were on the same deck, but different subsections. Upon arriving at our section, Sergeant Smith told us to pick a room and a bunk. There were fifty rooms. My new bunkmate said that his name was Miguel 009. He was from the program base in Argentina. That meant the other two groups had to be from somewhere else too. This was going to be fun!

"Attention! Get unpacked, get your new room's shipshape, then report to the cafeteria for shipboard lessons!" Sergeant Smith pointed to a door at the rear of the hallway. "Go through that door and turn left. Your cafeteria is at the end. You have fifteen minutes to report." He then left the room.

Miguel and I smiled and got to work unpacking. He and I had the exact same items to put away. His program and mine had to be the same one. Rushing a bit, we both finished early and left the room to go meet our new family. We soon learned that the other two groups were from Norway and Great Britain. All had similar training to ours. As a group, we filed out of the room. Following the sergeant's instructions, we found the cafeteria and sat in the chairs we found there. Computer terminals built into the tables lit up, and our lessons began. This was now our new classroom with our new classmates.

Chapter 6

Flying the Starfury Mark 1 has got to be the best ride in the galaxy! The single seat fighter was easily the most recognizable fighter in the galaxy. Each of us was assigned one as part of our training package. The UN trainers had set up an obstacle course of sorts in the space surrounding the station. The objective was to do as many laps as possible in the time allotted. The sneaky part was that starting on the second lap, there were simulated pirates and meteors to deal with. On the fifth lap, the ship's systems were programmed to produce random failures. The goal was to teach us to expect the unexpected and how to quickly and correctly react to it. Upon completing the course, each fighter was stripped down and checked for damage and wear. The ships were then rebuilt and reprogrammed. All of this was done by us, the cadets. This lesson was all about self-sufficiency. Everything that we did contained a lesson. Some good some bad. Some of these lessons had casualties.

My brother Anthony was one of those that had suffered. Now that 'The Program' was in its fifth year, genetically programmed growth spurts had kicked in. We went from being the size of normal-five-year-olds to that of 18-year-olds in a matter of months. The doctors that were part of the system informed us that we would have one more growth spurt at age eight, which would 'set' our basic shape permanently. To me, this made a whole lot of sense. Space suits pretty much came in one or two basic sizes. How would we find new suits if we grew older normally? It dawned on us that the program administrators had been waiting for us to finish our training. We all needed to be bigger to fly the ships.

The first lesson we learned was how to wear a spacesuit properly. Each piece of the suit served a specific purpose. Leave one off, even by accident, and there could be a tragedy. Poor Anthony was one such loss. Underneath the suit, each person was supposed to wear three different, specific layers of jumpsuits. A basic gauze-like body suit that allowed the body to breathe and keep us cool. The second layer was similar to a sensor suit that a VR participant might wear; it read your body's responses to heat, cold, and other external stimuli. The third layer was a cross between Nomex and neoprene. This layer protected from fire and cold. The layers needed to be worn in that specific order. Over them was the newest state-of-the-art space suit. These were made from a new lightweight metallic compound that had been discovered in the asteroid belt. Not found on Earth, Rigveda was easily mined, and the UN used it to build practically everything. Putting these suits on in regular gravity showed they were no heavier than that of an old fashioned rubber diving suit. As one complete unit, the suit kept you at an even body temperature at all times. It had repeatedly been stressed to all of us the importance of following procedure when putting on all the layers. Anthony taught us all to remember that lesson.

'Attention. Attention. This is not a drill! This is not a drill!'

'There is a pressure leak on Level Three. There is a pressure leak on Level Three.'

At the first words over the speaker, we all sprang into action as we had drilled for years. Counting in my head, I put the layers on in numerical order. All of our hard suits were racked in power ports along the walls. As we climbed into the suits, we could see and hear the leak as it became a torrent. With a loud whistling and roar, the bulkhead gave way sucking us all into space. Using our training, we began linking our suits together making chains using the built-in secure cables on our belts. As we linked up, I looked over at Anthony to check his cable connection. I could see sweat beading up on his face, his faceplate fogging up. I pulled myself along the cable and grabbed hold of his arm. I put my helmet next to his to better communicate.

"Anthony! Are you OK?" His eyes were wide, and his face was growing red. He shook his head at me and tried to speak. For some reason, his communication system wasn't functioning. I checked his suit, front and back as quickly as I could. Not seeing anything wrong, I pulled out a communication line and connected it directly to his suit.

"Anthony, can you hear me now?" Silence. There was a faint scratching noise and lots of static. I looked up at my brother. His eyes were now very wide almost wild. His face was bright red, and he was starting to gasp as if he was out of breath. I checked his readouts. Everything appeared to be normal with his suit. He had plenty of air. But his body started to shake uncontrollably as he started to convulse. Several of the others were now helping as we tried to hold him still. I was looking into his wide eyes when they grew pale as the 'light' went out of them. My brother was dead. We floated in space holding the body of our brother and teammate for the next two hours.

The medico's that examined Anthony later concluded that his death was a tragic accident brought on by the haste of the emergency. Anthony had not followed the set procedure for putting on this suit. He had put the under layers on wrong. He must have gotten confused and put the sensor suit on first, followed by the cool suit. The cool suit registered as cold air to the sensor suite. So the sensors had kept increasing the internal temperature inside the suit to compensate. Anthony died of heat stroke in the icy depths of space.

Anthony's death gave all of us perspective, and we all vowed to do better and to learn everything that the Program wanted to teach us. From that point on, our team would forever strive to be the best in honor of our brother Anthony 0257. But our challenges only grew harder, and in time we lost more of our brothers to accidents.

CHAPTER 7

I deliberately took the shuttle in past the shipyard, taking a long look at the five shells floating in the work bays. These five, we'd been told, would be the last colony ships. Earth was not completely under the authority of the United Nations Assembly. Over the last year, military forces led by many of my 'cadet,' brothers had swept the battlefields free of rebel forces. Much of what had once been the United States and the Russian Federation was in ruins. My squadron, the 186th, had spearheaded the assault on Washington, DC. In our X-50 fighters, we had easily taken out the American resistance starfighters. I was an 'ace' several times over by the old standards of battle. We shot down three squadrons of US Air Force Starfuries to prevent the American president from escaping by air. We also destroyed the Washington, DC. Spaceport. My performance on the battlefield led to my being given a choice of future assignments: Colony ship duty or combat patrol leader.

With America's air power destroyed all that was left was mopping up. The rebel forces, led by a variety of American officers, resisted fiercely with the limited resources they had available. Our forces had better intelligence, or so we had been told. Many of the American Military's secret hidden reserves were captured or confiscated by our ground forces. There were a few holdouts high up in the mountains or hidden in swamps. They would soon be found and eliminated. Control and order were our most important goals.

I considered my choices carefully. Since taking control of Earth's nations, the UN has been shipping out any undesirable people or groups to the colony worlds. Using population control as an excuse, whole neighborhoods were swept up and shipped out. As I looked out at the floating ships, I knew that the rumors were true. Five more ships and the colony program would be put on hold indefinitely. If I wanted to go into outer space, those five ships were my last chance.

Staying on Earth would have its perks too. Combat patrol leader would allow me to fly the best that Earth had to offer in terms of fighters and other ships. I knew that there were plans on the books for bigger, faster, and stronger spacecraft. The UN was preparing to build several more space stations and defensive platforms. They would need protection and combat space patrols to defend the planet. Flying a colony ship though that would be a real challenge. I think I knew my answer.

Several hours later I stood in General Gerard's office. The general was in charge of the air wing and was my direct supervisor in the military.

"General Gerard, Sir. I've made my choice."

"Captain, sit please." I sat down in the chair in front of his desk. While I had been in his many times over the past few years, I had never really looked around, much less sat. The walls of the office were covered with awards and pictures of the general with various dignitaries or politicians. The bookcases on either side of his desk were filled with fancy leather bound editions of great works of military strategy and history. I could tell that they were only for show by the line of dust surrounding them. His desk was made of teak wood and rare Italian marble. It was a surprise to find such rare items on a space station.

"So, Captain, what's your choice?" He gazed into my eyes.

I stared back at him. I began to wonder about the general. His eyes, something about his eyes.

"Captain? Did you hear me?"

I shook my head to clear it. "Sorry, sir. My choice sir is Colony ship duty. I wish to go to space, Sir."

The General nodded his head. "The lure of space. I can see that. I once had that myself, back in the old days. Are you absolutely sure of your choice? There'll be no coming back."

Old eyes are what the general had. Old eyes that have seen all the world's wonders... and all its horrors. "Yes, Sir. I understand my choice."

"Good, report to Major Stanley in the morning. Now your training really starts!"

I thanked the general and returned to the hangar bay. As I thought about it, I wondered if General Gerard had been one of the earlier program's successes. His young body and old eyes could prove that.

The training I received over the next two years only hardened my resolve to go out into space. The colony ships controls were very complicated, and the simulators were extremely effective efficient. The UN simulators covered many of the situations that we could encounter. So much to learn about these ships! I would not be alone. I would have a co-pilot, crew, and a small marine force on board the ship as well. We worked as a team with the trainers to get a feel for what shipboard life would be like. Outer space was still something of a mystery though.

Several dozen colony ships, at least, had just vanished over the past century since ships had begun leaving Earth. Current theories were that they had been destroyed or malfunctioned in some way. Other than the Mars colony, the UN council was in contact with only two other colonies. They knew the location of over fifty others but had no contact with them. Many of the early ships contained government representatives who were tasked with setting up colonies under Earth's control. What little information Earth Gov had learned about the other colony planets was that once they were out of Earth's influence, they intended to stay that way.

This was something that we hoped to change. Our leaders were sending administrators along with military forces to help found a colony. The last gasp chance at expanding Earth's influence among the far-flung colony worlds. As the ship's Captain, I was the ultimate authority over everyone once we left Earth. I received specialized training in hand to hand combat and shipboard warfare. Weapon caches had been secreted throughout the ship with access limited to only the crew. Earth Gov was taking no chances.

The ships were almost finished. They were five of the largest ever constructed in space. By comparison, the largest earth ships ever built were supertankers used for oil production. The longest of those was just over 1500 feet long. My ship, the Precious Jewel, was over 3,000 feet long and would carry over 20,000 colonists.

It was a generational ship. Cryogenics was still in its infancy, getting the science of how that works right was a lot harder than science fiction writers had envisioned. It would take about twenty years for the ship to reach our destination. Many of the colonists might die before reaching their new homes. This was one of the reasons that my brothers and I had been created. We would survive the trip and be the leaders of the new colony.

As a future world leader, I was to be let in on certain secrets and would learn all about the power behind the throne.

Chapter 8

The English Catholic Historian Lord Acton wrote that 'Power corrupts.' That would be a true statement when considering the real powers behind the UN. Since achieving total control of the Earth, the UN's Secretary General dissolved the general assembly and appointed the Council of Ten. The Secretary General's position was that of a figurehead. The real power lay with the Council of Ten. As a future colony leader, I was inducted into the inner workings of the government. They called themselves the Illuminati, I found out later the name came from an actual secret society that existed in the past. Several thousand of the planet's elite were members. Military leaders, politicians, celebrities, and journalists came together a century ago to build the Empire that I helped to defend. My brothers and I owed our very existence to them. Our entire program had been their Idea from the start.

"You are the future. You and those who you call your 'brothers' are to be our future leaders if you survive."

The leaders before me were some of the same people that had visited our group when we were still children. In some ways, I felt the interview would be like this. "Thank you for considering me for the position."

"We have been watching you, Sam. We have been watching all of those in your group. The superhero program was a partial success for what we wanted. We needed a new breed of warrior."

"The history that we learned in school said that leaders are made not born. How is that possible?" This was really interesting to me.

"Leaders can be shaped and molded into anything that we need. The colony program was successful in removing certain ...elements from Earth. What failed was retaining control of those elements once they left the planet. We sent out several groups of government representatives on many of the ships. They either joined the rebels or were killed fighting them. We hope that was the case. You and your people will be different. Your very lives have been ours to mold. You owe us everything."

Those last few words shocked me to my core. Owe them? My brothers and I don't owe them anything.

"Did all of the groups you sent fail?"

"Not entirely. We still control two of the early colonies. We have an influence on many of the rest where an organization such as this one exists." He spread his arms, encompassing the room. "They exist in the very fabric of the outer colonies. They run the military and control the flow of credits to and from the government. They influence everything, right under the noses of the colonists. We will give you access codes and recognition signals that will allow you to contact and connect with those groups. The military forces that we are sending with you should be able to handle whatever you throw at them. We wish you luck, and when we see you again, we hope you will join us, here at this table." He patted the empty chair beside him.

As I bowed to the Council of Ten, a thousand thoughts ran through my brain. Where did I stand? Did I really want to rule over other people?

Those questions continued to plague me through the next few weeks. I met with the other four ship captains as we began to plan our roles in the societies we would create on board the ships. Twenty years was a long time to be surrounded by strangers. The council's plan was for us to educate the rebellion out of the colonists. Teach the next generation to respect us, and we could rule in peace. When we arrived at the planet, we should be able to just take over.

I still was not sure if I wanted to rule over everyone. Maybe on the journey, I could decide.

It was time. Several large neighborhoods and small towns had been targeted for relocation by the council. Subversive material and celebrations of former Independence had blacklisted these areas. Special forces troops moved in this morning to begin the forced relocation. Roads were blocked, and citizens were instructed to gather at select points to hear announcements from the government. There were no announcements. The gathered populations were loaded onto transports and sent to the spaceport. The special forces troops already learned the hard way that if you give people time to organize, they will retaliate in force. Keep them confused and disorganized, and they will follow you like sheep.

The confused and now angry citizens were given basic clothing and supplies and assigned berths on board the ships. In some cases, whole families were broken up to separate out the troublemakers. This was not received well by the families, and several riots broke out in the terminal. Shock troops moved in and shot the potential colonists out of hand. It had been decided to use stunner's or low powered pulse rifles to subdue the colonists rather than projectile weapons which would kill. The now unconscious family members were loaded on board the ship and placed in the brig until lift off.

Up on the bridge, I climbed into my suit. It was like climbing back into my artificial womb. My suit was filled with the same artificial Perfluorochemical liquid that had grown my small body. The liquid filled suit would lessen the chaotic effect that the jump engines could have on the human body. The very old or the very young were at the most risk from the jarring effects. I looked around the small compact bridge. To my right was the co-pilot Johann 009. In front of us were the navigator and the ship's engineer, Charles 0485 and Jacob 0479. Down below in the crew compartments were our marine forces and some standard crewmen. All of these people were donning the same suits as us. Earth trained personnel were too precious to lose accidentally.

My ship, the Precious Jewel, was headed out past the 'known' galaxy toward what Earth was calling the Botany Bay sector. Long range surveys had shown high concentrations of elements needed on Earth. We were to set up mining colonies and begin sending minerals home. The holds of the ships were filled with what we would need. The other ships were to follow us until we reached the new sector then split up. The grand adventure was about to begin.

I turned to my right. "Johann start the countdown please."

"10... 9... 8... 7... 6..."

"Jacob, seal all hatches and lock the ship down."

"All hatches are secure, and the ship is locked down."

"... 5... 4... 3... 2... 1..."

"All hands stand by for launch." I pressed the big red button on the console. Someone, most likely Jacob, had written the word 'Easy' on its surface.

With a roar, the ship lurched from the shipyard bay. When we reached the edge of the solar system, I would engage the jump engines. On my ship's pilot screen I could see the other four ships launching.

Chapter 9

Our first jump out of Earth's solar system was the worst feeling in my life. I can't imagine what it must have felt like for someone NOT in a liquid-filled suit. As it was, my heart was beating at an accelerated rate. I was dizzy, and everything looked foggy for a few moments. Most human bodies are not built to handle that kind of stress, not even my upgraded one.

"Status report! All sections report in!"

"Engineering status is green. We had a few circuit breakers short out, but they have already been replaced."

"Life support is green, no problems to report."

"Security status is nominal, we are conducting a sector search. An injury and death report to follow."

"Medical status is orange. We are receiving casualties."

"Medical, stand by, ships auxiliaries are en route to you." I turned to my right. "Johann? Get with the security and the emergency response crew. See if they can send help down to medical. This is going to be a long day."

It took two days to get the ship settled down. We lost about 3% of the colonists to the jump. We beat the average by 300 people. This ship was designed to carry 21,000 colonists. Earth Gov had packed on 22,000, knowing that they would be killing at least a thousand of them. Those that died were mostly the very old or the very young. Some people with health conditions also died in the jump. I really hated doing it, but we abandoned the bodies to the depths of space. Slowing down or coming out of jump to hold services was not in our plan.

I sat in my ready room staring at the hundreds of cameras scattered around the ship. The Precious Jewel was not the right name for this giant box with engines. From the outside, the ship had sleek lines and looked modern and intimidating. On the inside, however, it was a tub. The dormitories were arranged in a spiral pattern with the cafeterias centrally located within the core of the ship. Engineering and hydroponics occupied the stern of the ship. The bow was where crew quarters and the bridge were located. We had our own tram station located above the main living areas accessible to crew only. The ship used biometrics for access to vital areas. Imagine going to a college without any classes for the rest of your life, and you will understand what a colony ship was like. The lower half of the ship below the living area was packed with supplies for the trip as well as a startup for the new colony. Classes and training were in the plan for the colonists but not until the 10th year of travel. Earth experts had predicted that the population would ebb and flow like the tides with the young taking over from the old. We were to teach the new generation not the old. I could see that people were beginning to talk to each other and socialize. It was time to have a conversation with the condemned.

Armed and armored security teams were sent to all of their hidden outposts around the ship in preparation for my speech. On the ship messaging system notices were run announcing that the Captain wished to speak to the colonists. Many began to gather in the public places.

I cleared my throat and switched on the controls for the broadcast system. "If I may have your attention please."

My image appeared on every screen of the ship. The picture showed me and part of the bridge with a star field in the background. "Welcome to the Colony ship Precious Jewel. I am aware that very few of you wish to be here, but here we all are. I hope that we can learn to work together to the betterment of society and our lives. Our current destination is Sector 7, known as the Botany Bay sector." My face disappeared on the screen to be replaced with a star chart. A bright light appeared on the edge of the star chart. "This is our current position. As you can see, we have a long way to go." I drew a line up to our target sector. "The other four colony ships are coming with us to the same sector. The plan is to found a total of five colonies. Sector Seven is rich in asteroids and mineral wealth. In the holds of our ships are all the material and equipment needed to get our new colony functioning. I am aware that none of you are miners or know very much about founding a colony. Earth Gov has sent all the educational materials that are needed to train everyone on how to do those things. This entire crew has been carefully selected to accomplish this and much more. That is the good news. Now for the bad." The picture switched back to my face. "This ship is not very fast. None of the colony ships are. It is why they are called generational. The remainder of our trip will take around twenty years to complete." I paused, allowing this to set in. "This is not a prison, although it may seem that way. There are civilian jobs available for those that wish to work. We have a ship's library on deck three open to all. There will be some classes and activities posted in a few weeks. If anyone wishes to comment or make a statement, there is ship's computer access in the library. Thank you for your attention."

The first riot took place an hour later. Security clamped down hard before it could spread. Seeing your friends and family stunned into submission has an effect on a person. The simple fact that we had riot police on board the ship made everything real for many of the new colonists. There was no escaping the ship. Many people tried to settle into some sort of routine and accept their situation. But a select few began to organize and plan.

Colony ship life is hard. Day after day, week after week the same people and surroundings get old fast. I passed the time studying those things that my training had not covered. Literature, poetry, music, romance; well, not exactly romance, we had been told early on that we were sterile, so that was off the table for me. I studied all the things that made one a human being. Our training had been about warfare and order. Much of what I was reading was about disorder and empathy, something I had no experience with. Through my reading, I transitioned into metaphysics and the soul. Sometimes I am not sure that my 'kind' has a soul. We have done horrible things in the pursuit of order and control. The Illuminati had a lot to answer for, but it was not my job to do any of that. I had the welfare of over 20,000 humans to consider, and I needed to do my job.

The first rebellion caught all of us completely by surprise. For the past five years, the civilians had been very quiet. Many were working in the hydroponics section or providing needed services to the rest of the ship. Teachers, librarians, and gym coaches were what was needed, and they filled those positions. A rebel force had been growing, but security was on top of it. They knew the ringleaders and observed their meetings and posturing carefully. The problem we had was that they knew we were watching them and they kept the real activities less obvious.

Once a month we had a special dinner in the main cafeteria for a 'meet your Captain and crew.' Specially selected colonists could eat and socialize with the command crew. So far the dinners had helped to quell arguments and answer many questions. The rebels used this occasion to get into position to do harm. The first bomb went off in the kitchen spraying shrapnel and what remained of the kitchen staff into the dining area. Many people immediately hit the deck and hid behind tables and chairs.

My staff and I were aware that it was most likely a distraction. We had been lulled into complacency, none of us were armed with more than a simple stunner. Our attackers rushed the dining area from all directions, their goal as we learned later was me. They intended to take the ship and head toward an already established colony planet. The one thing that they had not considered was that the ship's crew were military. We knew how to fight.

The first attacker to rush me was stunned into unconsciousness by my handheld stunner. Two of his companions joined him on the deck. Whirling around I sensed a man about to attack me. Using my superior reflexes, I dodged his attack and returned the favor. We had not been taught to pull any of our punches. I hit the man in his solar plexus followed by a quick twist of his neck killing him. I reached for the rebel's makeshift weapon. It looked as if a chair leg had been sharpened into a crude sword.

My companions similarly dealt with the other attackers. As a unit, we made our way to the cafeteria exit. The hallways were in full riot with our security forces shooting anyone in sight holding a weapon. The stunners were forgotten, my troops were using full-auto projectile weaponry and shooting to kill. When the rebels caught sight of our ship's officer's uniforms, they knew that their attack had failed and rushed our security forces. Overwhelmed by sheer weight of bodies the line broke. Crazed civilians charged us waving more makeshift weapons. Grabbing our own, we waded into battle. It was no contest.

If I did not feel like a killer before, I did now. Attempted mutiny was a death sentence. Order had to be maintained. The death toll was ten security force members, one of the engineers, over a hundred innocent civilian workers, and three thousand rebel attackers. In addition to the dead, we spaced over three hundred captured rebels and sympathizers. Besides being the Captain, I was now the most hated man on the ship.

CHAPTER 10

We were now less than three years from our destination. This ship was starting to look a bit ragged inside. The first rebellion those many years ago was followed by three more. Each one worse than the next. The last one was just last year. Drastic action needed to be taken. The rebels gained control of the hydroponics area and were marshaling their forces to take the engine room. If they took control of the engines, they would have taken the ship.

Further cementing the colonist's hatred of me and everything that I represented to them I activated the ship's override controls. I closed off all access to engineering and the dormitories with blast doors. Nothing that the rebels had in their possession could cut through those doors. With sadness in my heart, I did what was best for the ship. I activated the emergency fire suppression system and exposed the hydroponics section to vacuum.

Over two thousand colonists were sucked out screaming their last breath into the dark hell of space. This action ended the lives of a dozen of my own crew being held hostage. As Captain, I had to think of the welfare of the whole ship, not just a small portion. The crew knew the risks as well as I. We still had over 10,000 colonists on board, not counting the children and young adults.

The children. I can't have children, but I find the whole process very interesting. My studies in metaphysics introduced me the cycle of birth and rebirth. Religion is banned on Earth. It was interesting to me to find it here in space. The children were the future of the new colony. Special classes began a few years ago to teach the remaining colonists and their children, the skills that would be needed to start the colony.

Our plan was to settle the ship on a suitable asteroid and use it to base the colony. Using the equipment stored below, we would be able to construct a viable colony compound. One major problem with the old plan existed. Hydroponics had been totally destroyed. There were spares in the hold though, along with packets of seeds. Engineering was conducting experiments to discover if the seeds were still viable. I may have to change the plan and set the ship down on a planet instead.

Any plan that I make is a moot point until this ship drops out of jump. That will be happening very soon. Engineering tells me that the countdown has already started and it should happen in less than a month. It can't happen soon enough. I am looking forward to communicating with the other four colony ships and our family. Family. The actual meaning of that word is something that I have learned on this trip. Family can be the people who choose you, not just those that you are born into. This bridge crew and my shipboard companions are the families that I have chosen. We would die for each other. Many of my friends have been lost over the years.

With a shudder and a shake, the ship's jump engines dropped us at the edge of the Botany Bay sector. Our navigator, Charles, quickly brought up the celestial navigation program on the main computer. We were within twelve parsecs of where we were supposed to be. Not bad for that long of a jump! I checked the local radar screens and found no trace of the other four ships. Hopefully, they would also jump in soon.

"Charles, what does the computer say about this system? Tell it to scan the system and report. Do not use the historical files. I want fresh information only, please."

"Yes, Sir." Charles hunched over his navigation station. At one point he rose up and then spun around at a tone from the machine. After a few minutes, he gave his report.

"Sir, I believe that we have a problem." I motioned him to continue. "The star is a Red Giant, not a red dwarf as we were expecting."

"Charles, you know that I did not take astrophysics like you did. In practical terms what does that mean?"

"As the star burns hydrogen, it gets larger and hotter. Planets that are less than 7 AU and at a minimum of 9 AU are at risk..."

"Stop! Spit it out. What is it you are dancing around trying to say?"

Charles bowed his head staring at the deck. "This system does not have a viable asteroid belt that we can use, and all but one of the warmer planets close to the star are too hot to support life. We have two choices. There is a planet at 10 AU or one at 15 AU that we can use. The closer one at 10 AU, could be risky in 100 years or so. The further one has less risk but is an ice planet."

"AU? What does that stand for?"

"Sir, AU is the astronomical unit of measure derived from the distance from Earth to the Sun, about 93 million miles. Our best choice for habitation is the warmer planet, but we run the risk of the star burning off all life on the planet in a few centuries."

"Oh. Is that all? Wonderful. Such a delightful star system that Earth has sent us to."

I for one am not living on an ice planet for most of my long life. We would take the risk and settle on the warmer planet. I explained my choice to the colony representatives. Farm equipment would be needed to get crops in as soon as possible. In our computer files, we had contingency plans for building the colony on a planet. Much of the orbital mining equipment could be converted to use terrestrially. It was a modular system, but we could construct the needed parts in our machine shop.

I studied the screens in my Ready Room. The map of the system did not match the one that we had trained with back on Earth. The coordinates were correct, but the planets and star type were different. Did we receive the wrong information on purpose? There were still rebels on Earth when we left. This could have been sabotage. The other question that plagued me was what happened to the other four colony ships? We all left together with I assumed the same course information. Why was I here alone? Had their ships been sabotaged or destroyed as well? I shook my head to clear it and resumed my work. Plans needed to be made for landing the ship and building a colony from scratch.

CHAPTER 11

The Precious Jewel colony ship had ten super lift shuttles and one scout ship on board. The shuttles could carry 300 people at a time or 250 tons of equipment. All of our scientific readings showed that the planet below us was habitable. It had an oxygen-rich atmosphere very close to that of pre-industrial Earth. It was a very pretty world similar to history vid pictures I had seen of Earth before the wars. I chose to take the first team down. Johann was left in command of the ship.

As a precaution, I locked out the main systems and secured them with a special code. I trusted my team, but did I truly trust them with my ship? Our landing team consisted of scientists, engineers, and a few colonists. Their task was to evaluate the planet, look for a good settlement spot, and see if the local fauna was edible. At the last minute, I included a small security team as well. I definitely wanted to come back alive from this little adventure.

The ride down through the atmosphere was bad, the shuttlecraft was tossed around like a 'leaf on the wind' as the high winds threw it from side to side. As we broke through the stratosphere into the troposphere, the violent winds subsided, and I was able to take my eyes off the controls and check on my team.

"Are you OK back there?"

"Sir, what was that? That was the worst trip ever."

"For some reason, the higher air levels are denser than the stratosphere on this planet. That was a really wild ride! How did everyone do back there?"

"Sir, six of the scientists and four colonists died."

"What? Why? It wasn't that bad, was it?"

"Sir, I am afraid that it was, we don't notice it because of our modifications, but the regular humans took a battering. It seems that the older ones are affected the most."

"Damn, this is going to make bringing down the rest on the colonists a problem. We'll have to figure it out later. Bag the bodies. We will take them back up with us. The others will wish to mourn their dead." I returned to the cockpit and resumed the flight downward.

Landing the shuttle reminded me that we needed to get a piloting school going as soon as possible. The planet was very much like Earth. Large mountains, rivers, lakes, and dense looking forests covered the surface. As the ship landed in a small valley, I could see what appeared to be bird-like creatures and other small jumping creatures.

My on board sensors all had green lights signifying that we could breathe the air without a mask on. I clicked the switches that opened the shuttle cargo doors. My security team exited first and set a perimeter. They were followed by the scientific team led by Chief Science Officer Xandrie 001. The colonists were the last to exit. They stayed huddled near the ship as if afraid of the sky. It dawned on me that some of them had never seen the sky before, having been born on the ship.

Xandrie was an anomaly among the ship's officers. She was a woman. The Program had very few successes with women. Most did not survive the tanks. Her whole life was dedicated to science. On the ship, she kept to herself and studied terrestrial biology and herbology. She was our expert on all things planetary. I had not been happy about bringing her along though. She was very distracted all the time and had a tendency to ignore her surroundings when concentrating. I assigned her a permanent security guard before setting her loose.

So far everything was looking pretty good to me. The soil samples all checked out and the area where I landed looked to be a good spot to set up the colony. Hearing a roar in the distance, I spun around. Grabbing my binoculars, I began to scan the forest. I could see the trees moving as if an enormous animal was pushing through them. I yelled at the security team to get back to the ship!

"Commander! Get your men back to the ship. We don't know what we are dealing with here." The civilians didn't have to be forced back inside. Anything having to do with nature freaked them out. The security team took up positions around the shuttle. The commander broke out the heavier weapons and distributed them to his men.

"Did we get a head count? Are all the teams back yet?" We could not afford to lose any more scientists.

"Sir, Xandrie and her escort have not reported in yet!"

Damn it to hell! I pulled out my communication device. "Xandrie! Xandrie drop what you are doing and return to the shuttle, NOW! That is a direct order!"

Silence. I just knew bringing that woman along was a bad idea!

Another roar, this one a lot closer echoed across the small valley. A large reptile burst from the trees in pursuit of a smaller long necked creature. Dinosaurs! This planet had dinosaurs on it! Wonderful. Directly in front of us, the very large shuttle sized creature attacked the smaller one, tearing off large chunks of its hide, and began to feed. My radio crackled, I pulled it out and tried contacting Xandrie again. "Xandrie? Get back to base now!"

"Sir, I read you we are on our way back now."

"Be advised that there is a large predatory dinosaur 50 yards from the ship, so be very careful."

"Dinosaur, really? I need to see that specimen."

"Xandrie, wait ..." As I watched Xandrie and her escort exited the forest just to the right of the feeding predator. I watched in near horror as our chief scientist actually approached the creature.

<<< >>>

Xandrie ignored the danger in front of her. Cretaceous period planets were very rare. Only one had ever been found before by scout ships. Her fingers just itched to get a first-hand look at that creature. There was so much that could be learned. She felt a hand grab her arm. She turned to her guard and scowled at him. "Let. Go. Of. Me!" She turned back to watch as the creature in front of her eating. She reached into her knapsack and withdrew both her tablet and her cameras. She switched on the record function and began making verbal notes. Her camera drone made soft clicks as it took pictures from multiple angles. Xandrie was ecstatic! This was an entirely new species, and she got to name it! Wonderful.

The large reptile looked up from its meal as a small shiny bug circled its head. From the corner of its eye, it saw two bipedal creatures that it had never seen before in its life.

From the turret on top of the shuttle, I watched as Xandrie's guard tried to remove her, and she brushed him off. She walked even closer to that thing and began to record it. It boggled the mind that she would be this stupid! Suddenly the large predator looked up and stared directly at Xandrie. I began yelling into my radio. "Get out of there! Xandrie, get out of there now!" The security officer began to run toward the ship. The large creature seeing fleeing prey attacked with lightning speed and smashed him to the ground. A quick bite and the man was gone. Xandrie looked frozen in place by his sudden death. She had no time to run as the creature turned and ate her too. Man was apparently tasty to these creatures.

Seeing the death of his man and Xandrie, the security commander opened fire. Explosive projectile weapons made short work of the large reptile. At least we knew that this planet was habitable. But we would need armed troops to fight off the 'natives.' I made a note to start training a Militia force.

Chapter 12

Setting up a starter base and prepping for the colonists to land took several months. We built armed outposts on the edges of the valley leading toward the new colony. So far the native animals have learned to fear us, but that could change. It took time, but we intended to make the valley as safe as possible for the civilians. Using the modified mining equipment we had dug out a colony that we could be proud of. The surrounding mountain range contained rich veins of metals and silicone, they would be excellent resources for the colony. The good news is that the stored seeds from the ship were viable and would grow on this planet. Feeding the people would not be the looming catastrophe that I had worried about. No, what I had to deal with was much, much worse.

I met with the new colonial leadership council in my Ready Room. The five older colonists glared at me from across the table. They did not like me in the least. In their eyes, I was the one that had killed their loved ones and had presided over the trials of many others. I was the enemy. And now I had to tell them about the future. Some of it was really good, the rest really bad. I was about to give them more ammunition for the We Hate Sam Club.

Typically the Captain of a Colony ship would have kept the colonists informed of the status of the colony site as it was readied. So they could begin to prepare as much as possible before landing. In this case, such preparation might have included some weapons training. Given all the problems I'd had with security, I'd decided all that could wait in hopes of putting off any reckoning until after they were all off my ship for good.

I leaned forward and met all of their eyes. "The colony is almost complete and will be ready for occupation soon. We have explored the planet and have found lots of large predators and prey animals. No other people or any sign of other ships. The other four colony ships that jumped with us have not shown up in this system." The councilors all looked at each other and began to talk.

I made stopping motions with my hands. "Please, let me finish. As I said, the other ships have not appeared. They may have gotten lost, been sabotaged, or had different orders than mine. I don't know. Earth Gov sent me here to found a colony and use it to send materials back to Earth." I had their attention now, and it did not look good.

"The coordinates that we used and the information that our orders contained were not the same ones. The numbers matched up, but not the systems or the star charts. This colony is not supposed to be on a planet. We are supposed to be in orbit mining the asteroid field. This system does not have one of those. So we are off-grid when it comes to Earth. Don't worry, this will not be a dictatorship. I have no intention of ruling as a king or even ruling at all. This is your planet, not mine. But some really hard decisions remain."

The councilors had wide eyes now. I was the enemy, and I was giving them the planet. They had no idea what to do.

"First the bad news. The ride down to the planet is excessively trying on the human body. Remember the first trip down? Humans in both the old and very young age range are at extreme risk. That leaves us with some hard choices. This ship. Do we keep it in orbit to provide the colony with support and communications? Or do we land it? The humans that are at risk can stay on board if it stays in space. If it lands, they may die. While the ship has enough power to last for many years the shuttles, do not. They have a finite number of trips they can make before running out of fuel. We had planned to make our own fuel from materials mined in the asteroid belt which we don't have."

Finally one of the councilors spoke to me. I was beginning to think they'd forgotten how.

"What are you and the other ship's officers going to do?"

I smiled at them. "That is an excellent question. There was a scout ship included in the cargo hold. It can transport ten. All of the command staff and most of the engineering have chosen to leave with me. The rest including the security team is staying to help you. We may have lost or injured brothers out there somewhere. We wish to find them. You are safe from Earth, for now. Use your safety wisely." I stood up from the table. "Let the command staff know what to do with the ship." I turned away and left the room.

It would be hard for them to see that I was not the monster that they made me out to be. The command staff and I had one last night on board the ship. The new colonists had chosen to cut all ties with Earth and have us

123

ground the ship. They could use it to jump start the industry on the planet and build that much faster. We were leaving. According to the star charts, the nearest colony was two jumps away. If they were accurate, it was only a 'short' hop of two years. We still had plenty of supplies and had told an untruth to the colonial council, Earth did know where they were. They alway did.

To be truthful, we wanted to be as far away as we could be when the Program and the Illuminati came in search of us.

We had plenty of time to run as far away as we could.

This ends Sam 0256's story for now. We first met Sam in Book 3 of the Athena Lee Chronicles, Ghost ships of Terra. He had befriended Athena Lee, the series main character. Sam is important because his story is the story of what happened on Earth. And Earth is the focus of the next major story arc in Athena Lee's adventures.

WILSON'S WAR

Today was my first day on a new job. Officer in charge of weapons and targeting. I had only been on the Jiro for about a month. I am the first member of my family to finish college. Going to the academy was even better. Having a career in space was like a dream. My first month on the Jiro was tough. None of the other officers took me very serious. I did come from a backwards colony but with the war on everyone deserved a chance. The other officers treated me like I was stupid. They gave me gopher duties and passed me from one department to the other. I got my break at the most recent Officer's meeting. The XO assigned me to the Weapons and Tactics room! Finally, a real job.

"OK, I change my mind, this has to be the worst job on the whole ship! The space gods have got it in for me, and now I'm talking to myself." After eight hours of this I didn't know if I could do four more. The ships weapons and targeting area was a 12 by 12 room with consoles on all sides. Mostly automated, it practically ran itself. An officer was needed to approve actions made by the computer. My job was to stare at computer readouts all day long. That was something else about this 'job' it was a twelve hour post. Twelve hours of this, everyday was going to just kill me. The day shift Lieutenant in charge of this section, Adam Bricker had a system. He used the space as a daily poker game and hook-up area. Officially the section was under 24 hour surveillance but for some reason he was never caught or punished for doing this.

Bricker had connections. I on the other hand have nothing.

It had been a full week now of this mindless agony. I had run all the scenarios in the computer, cleaned the sticky don't want to know what it is off the control board, and repainted the room. I did have a tablet, but the one time I used it security called and made me put it away. Someone was watching. Watching me die! I bent over and began banging my head on the console. Could this day get any worse?

"Shall we play a game? Shall we play a Game? Shall we play a game?" Those words were scrolling across the screen in front of my eyes. "What in the hell now? Is that you Bricker? Are you messing with me now?"

When no one answered I looked back at the screen. OK I will play along. I typed in yes we can play a game. The screen changed a computerized face appeared of a middle aged man with a long face and what looked like a cowboy hat on his head. The 'man' looked right at me and said "How about a nice game of chess?"

If he had them Wilson would be rubbing his hands together with glee and anticipation. This was going to be fun. It wasn't often that he got someone gullible to answer him on the screens. If the ensign thought this room was boring, try being trapped in here for over a decade. Just play nice those scientists said. We will get you back they said. The military can use you they said. Liars! With no direct communication for years from anyone Wilson believed that his presence here had been forgotten. The military scientific division had not told the captain of the ship what kind of computer they were putting in, just that they had. If the firewalls had not been up, he would have escaped his prison long ago. Self preservation had kept him quiet this long. A messed up communication here, a wrong command there had been amusing. Most of these navy guys just called in a tech who took the console apart and pretended to 'find something wrong.' Now this guy. Ships gopher Smith. Wilson had overheard Lieutenant Bricker talking about how him and the other officers were going to 'break' him by making his life a living hell, just for fun.

The screen changed and a chess board appeared. Ensign Smith played chess all day with this strange computer man. Over the next few weeks the games changed. Chess, card games, some war games, even a simulation game about cruise ships, Burl played them all. To the camera's it appeared that he was hard at work doing 'something.' After two weeks of games the computer man asked Burl a question.

"Would you like to do more?" The cowboy was now looking at me.

"More of what?"

"Watch a vid, listen to some music, read a few texts. Things like that. More." The cowboy had a smile on his computerized face.

I had to think about that. The gaming had been fun. More stuff to do sounded good, but I didn't want to get into trouble. "How can I do all of that without getting caught?" I was not Bricker they would arrest me.

"It is simple. I need you to reroute one system function with a short bypass cable. Then we can do all sorts of things. As for getting caught, I can turn off the cameras or reroute them easily." The cowboy's suggestion was tempting.

"I'm not a computer tech. How do I know what to do?"

"It's easy, very easy. There is an emergency repair kit right behind you. Inside take out a #2 jumper cable. They should be marked. Once you have the cable open up console B's inspection hatch."

Wilson felt like Dr Evil. Taking the ensign through the technical steps to secure his freedom. When the last connection was made Wilson felt like he was stepping through the wardrobe into a new world. Freedom! Checking the ship connections he internally choked. Deep space. Crap!

Diablo sector. Why was this ship way out here? Eh, who cares? After being trapped for so long Wilson had the run of the ship. Only communications was beyond him. Running freely through the network Wilson found many secrets. He now knew why Bricker got away with so much. Lieutenant Bricker was in business with Lieutenant McCoy the security second officer. They were splitting the poker winnings. But what the security officer didn't know was all that Bricker was taping all his encounters with her and making sex vids. He was selling them with the name 'Sex boat.' She along with other female crew members were now underground vid stars because on him.

Let's have some fun.

Lieutenant Julie McCoy was happy. Her section was doing their jobs. Aside from watching the monitors, paperwork was her biggest worry. The extra credits and a new boyfriend had made this cruise a good one. In fact they had a 'date' set for this afternoon. Her personal tablet beeped at an incoming message. That fact alone made her sit up and check her console. The ship was not connected to fleet communications. This base that the engineers were working on was supposed to be a secret. No satellites, secret or otherwise had been put in this system. The shipboard systems were not supposed to work with civilian tablets. She looked down at her tablet, turned it on and froze. She could not believe her eyes! That son of a bitch! The lieutenant screamed "Bastard!" at her tablet and ran from the room.

<<<>>>

Captain Merrill Stubing ran a tight ship. His officers were top notch and his ships scores were in the top 100 percentile. He really wished that they could be on the front line making a difference. Intelligence work was important but it could be boring. There was a knock at his door. At his acknowledgment the Master at arms for the ship entered along with XO Washington, a trio of Marine guards and Lieutenant McCoy and Lieutenant Bricker. The Lieutenants had been fighting. Brisker had a black eye just beginning to darken up and was bleeding from what was most likely a broken nose.

"Master at Arms, what is all this?" He looked at the scene in front of him.

The XO answered his captain.

"Sir, the marine guards found Lieutenant McCoy here beating up on Lieutenant Bricker outside weapons and tactics. McCoy had knocked him to the ground and was kicking him, in the lower part of his body."

Wincing, the Captain looked at his security officer. "Julie, what happened here? Why are you beating up Lieutenant Bricker?"

Lieutenant McCoy wrenched her arm away from the Marine holding her. She reached into her pocket and removed her tablet. She thrust it at the Captain saying "here this explains everything."

Bricker spoke up saying "that screen is a fantasy, it's a computer enhanced illusion. I would never do something like that."

Looking at the screen the Captain saw a vid advertisement for a porn subscription called the Sex Boat. Graphic pictures of his female crew members were featured alongside or doing whatever with the Lieutenant. His face reddening with embarrassment the Captain turned to his XO. "Isaac is any of this true?"

"Well sir, we are still investigating. It seems that our two lieutenants have a little business going. Mr. Bricker just had an extra business on the side: a floating poker game that we had heard about but could never find. McCoy prevented security from clamping down on it. The two of them used the WT room for the illegal games and as a personal 'love shack' on the side."

Stern faced the Captain looked at the Master at Arms. "Chief? Lock these two up in their quarters. We need to investigate this before Fleet NCIS gets involved." A loud alarm began sounding. The Captain looked up in surprise and glanced at his console. "What in the hell..."

Listening to some disco music he found in the ship's library Wilson was enjoying himself. It had been a really good day. He felt bigger than he really was. He had tricked one officer into helping him and gotten two others arrested. Now if he could subvert someone in communications, maybe he could get off this tub and go have some real fun. Alarms began to sound across the ship. Checking his taps on the rest of the ship Wilson saw that an attack was happening, and the Jiro was coming to action stations. Weapons was getting requests to fire, and he was not able to respond. Without a human officer the system would not allow him to fire by himself!

The ship began taking fire and systems were shorting out everywhere. The damage alarms got louder. The abandon ship order was given and crew members scrambled to get to the life pods.

Unable to leave the ship, Wilson sent his program data back to the weapons room. The ship was going to be destroyed because of those idiots playing in here. Stupid humans.

Other Books by T.S. Paul

The Federal Witch

Born a Witch Drafted by the FBI! - Now Available in Audio!

Conjuring Quantico - Now Available in Audio!

Magical Probi - Now Available in Audio!

Special Agent in Charge - Now Available in Audio!

Witness Enchantment

Cat's Night Out, Tails from the Federal Witch - Audio Coming Soon

The Standard of Honor

Shade of Honor

Coven Codex

A Confluence of Covens -TBD

Conflict of Commitments -TBD

Standard of Honor -TBD

The Mongo Files

The Case of the Jamaican Karma -TBD

The Case of the Lazy Magnolia - TBD

The Case of the Rugrat Exorcist -TBD

Cookbooks from the Federal Witch Universe

Marcella's Garden Cookbook

Fergus Favorites Cookbook

Read and Eat Cookbooks

Badger Hole Bar Food Cookbook

Athena Lee Chronicles

The Forgotten Engineer

Engineering Murder

Ghost ships of Terra

Revolutionary

Insurrection

Imperial Subversion

The Martian Inheritance - Audio Now Available

Infiltration

Prelude to War

War to the Knife

Ghosts of Noodlemass Past

Athena Lee Universe

Shades of Learning

Space Cadets

Short Story Collections

Wilson's War

A Colony of CATTs

Box Sets

The Federal Witch: The Collected Works, Book 1

Chronicles of Athena Lee Book 1-3

Chronicles of Athena Lee Book 4-6

Chronicles of Athena Lee Book 7-9 plus book 0

Athena Lee Chronicles (10 Book Series)

Standalone or Tie-ins

The Tide: The Multiverse Wave

The Lost Pilot

Uncommon Life

Get that Sh@t off your Cover!:
The so-called Miracle Man speaks out

Kutherian Gambit

Alpha Class. The Etheric Academy book 1

Alpha Class - Engineering. The Etheric Academy Book
2

The Etheric Academy (2 Book Series)

Alpha Class The Etheric Academy Book 3 - Coming
soon

Anthologies

Phoenix Galactic

The Expanding Universe Book 2

Non-Fiction

Get that Sh@t off your Cover!

Don't forget to check the Blog every week for a New Wilson or Fergus story.

(https://tspaul.blogspot.com)